UP
PERISCOPE

By ROBB WHITE

Frontispiece by Charles Beck

SCHOLASTIC BOOK SERVICES

Published by Scholastic Book Services, a division
of Scholastic Magazines, Inc., New York, N.Y.

For
M. T.

Copyright © 1956 by Robb White. Copyright © 1960 by Scholastic Magazines, Inc. This Scholastic Book Services edition is published by arrangement with Doubleday & Company, Inc.

6th printing.................................January 1965

Printed in the U.S.A.

PART I—SUBMARINE

CHAPTER 1

KENNETH M. BRADEN, LIEUTENANT (junior grade), U.S. Naval Reserve, sat perfectly still and waited for the admiral to finish talking on the telephone.

From his chair Ken Braden could look down on Hawaii's Pearl Harbor. The battleship *California* was lying, broken, her decks awash. The *Oklahoma* had capsized. Only the *Nevada's* bow was above water. Other ships were rusting, burned-out hulks as a result of the Japanese sneak attack on that Sunday morning almost two years ago. All around the harbor, and on Ford Island in the middle of it, there were signs of bomb damage and fire.

In spite of all the wreckage and ruined ships there was movement everywhere in the harbor. Ships of all sorts were coming and going or lay tied up at the wharves. On Ford Island, Navy battle planes were landing or taking off—Ken could even see a jeep with a big red sign on the back reading FOLLOW ME scurrying around. And everywhere there was the flickering, hard, bright blink of welding as the damage of war was repaired.

Close outside the window some myna birds were making a surprising amount of noise as they fought among themselves on the green lawn. But somehow here

1

in the room with the admiral everything was quiet—waiting.

The admiral kept on talking on the phone. Ken at last crossed his legs, the khaki trousers so starched and firmly pressed that they rattled a little as he moved.

He glanced again at the chart on the wall. In big letters above it were the words TOP SECRET. Below them, in smaller letters, was SUBMARINE DISTRIBUTION CHART-PACIFIC OCEAN AREA.

On the pale blue chart there were little flags with names on them, and tiny models of submarines floated here and there.

The names of the islands on the chart were strange, some harsh, some soft—Eniwetok, Ujelang, Rongelap, Nukuoro.

Strange names; strange, dangerous, distant places in the wastes of the Pacific.

The admiral kept on talking and Ken, sitting there waiting, wondered again what he had gotten himself into.

Weeks ago—in California—he had volunteered for what the commanding officer of the Underwater Demolition School had called only a "job." There hadn't been any details about it, just a "job," but Ken and a lot of the other students had held up their hands.

But nothing had happened. Weeks went by and no more was said about it. Until—in the middle of the night —a messenger woke him up. In two hours he was in a plane. In a few more hours he was in Hawaii.

And now, still knowing nothing about the "job," he waited.

Ken heard the admiral ask, "What boats are available?" Someone on the other end of the phone answered and the admiral frowned. "Only *Wahoo* and *Shark*, eh? Then it'll have to be *Shark*."

Another pause and the admiral said, "It'll *have* to be

Shark, Bill. I'm sorry." Then he hung up and turned back to Ken.

For half an hour before the phone call the admiral had been talking to him. Just chatting. Where had he gone to college? How long had he been in the Navy? How old was he? How much did he weigh?

The admiral had not yet even hinted to Ken the reason for his being here; the reason for the quick, secret flight from California.

Instead the admiral went on chatting. Asking questions. "What sports did you go out for in college, Braden?"

"Boxing, sir, and lacrosse."

"Not swimming?"

Ken tried to smile. "No, sir. I never was much of a swimmer."

"Oh. . . . Were you a good boxer?"

"We had a good trainer, sir. He kept us in shape and it showed up in our fights with other schools."

The admiral sat down on the corner of his desk and began tapping the side of his shoe with a long wooden pointer. "How many fights did you lose?"

"None, sir."

"Tell me," the admiral said, "when you volunteered for this job, did they let you know that it was not going to be a picnic?"

"They just said it was a job, sir."

"How many of you volunteered for it?"

"A lot, sir."

"Any idea why the commanding officer chose you, Braden?"

"No, sir. I wasn't the best underwater man in my class or anything like that."

The admiral tapped his shoe. "Twenty-two of you volunteered, Braden. Tell me, do you remember a girl you met on Shell Beach at La Jolla?"

Ken hesitated, then remembered. Sally . . . Sally John-

3

son? Jenkins? A blonde. Good-looking. Had a brother in the Navy. "Yes, sir."

"She asked you a lot of questions."

"She was interested, sir. She had a brother in the Navy."

The admiral nodded. "And do you remember a man who gave you a lift to Port Hueneme one Sunday?"

"Yes, sir."

"He asked a lot of questions, too."

Ken nodded.

"From the time you volunteered for this job, Braden, until right now you have met a good many people, been asked a good many questions. So did all the others who volunteered. Now I'll tell you something. All the people you met—the girl at La Jolla, the man who gave you a lift, all of them—were security agents. They asked questions to see if you would answer. You didn't. Of the twenty-two volunteers you were the only one who didn't fail the security test. That's why you were chosen."

Instead of making Ken feel proud, it made him feel cold. Whatever it was, it must be big. They wouldn't waste time like that if it weren't.

"Tell me," the admiral said, "when you were a kid were you always getting into fights with the other kids?"

Ken tried again to smile. "No, sir. I don't think I ever had a fight."

"Then you're not very belligerent?"

"I guess not, sir."

The admiral stopped tapping his shoe. "Did you volunteer for this job because your father is a prisoner of the Japanese?"

"That had a lot to do with it, sir. We haven't heard anything about him except that he survived the death march from Corregidor."

"Your father's an Army doctor, isn't he?"

"Yes, sir."

"My brother's in the Army, too. He made that death

march with your father—and lived. But I don't know whether he's still alive. I'm going to find out—with your help, perhaps."

The admiral walked over to the chart on the wall and tapped the blue Pacific with a pointer. "All right. All I can tell you about this job is that—if you still want it—it is going to be hard, lonely, and dangerous." He tapped the chart. "Out here."

Ken nodded.

"It is also important," the admiral said, pulling a cloth across to completely conceal the chart. "You could lose your life."

Then he turned around. "Think it over for a while and then let me know. There won't be any medals for you. Nobody will even know whether you're a hero or not. It's just a risky, dirty job which, if you pull it off, will save some lives, save some ships."

Ken started to say something, but the admiral stopped him. "If your answer is 'no' I'll understand that and think none the less of you for it."

Ken tried to imagine what the job might be but all he could think about was the huge, blank Pacific Ocean.

The admiral seemed to want him to say something so, at last, Ken said, "How would I—I mean, anybody—get out there, Admiral?"

"Submarine."

Ken couldn't stop the shiver going up his spine. "Oh," he said.

The admiral put the pointer down. "Go think it over, Braden. And, no matter what your decision is, there must be no discussion with anyone about it, nor about what we've talked of this morning. I don't want anybody to know who you are, where you came from, what your training has been. As far as you know, you're just another j.g. in the officers' pool waiting assignment. If you talk it may cost you your life."

Ken stood up. "Aye, aye, sir." His khakis cracked a little as he went out.

For a moment the admiral stood in the empty room looking at the door Ken had closed behind him. Then he spoke into a squawk box on his desk. In a moment a commander came in carrying a thin sheaf of papers in a folder.

From the window the admiral watched Ken Braden walking slowly down the hill.

Without turning from the window the admiral said, "There's the man we want, Bill. But does he want the job?"

"Good boy?" the commander asked.

"Yes. Quiet. Steady. Not the hero type. He's got a reason, too. His father's a Jap POW."

"I didn't see him when he came in," the commander said.

"He's got a good chin," the admiral said. "Good, level eyes. Big, honest mouth. Weighs one sixty; close to six feet. Boxed in school. Won. He was scared in here, not nervous."

"Sounds good. Here's the *Shark's* patrol report, sir."

The admiral turned back to the desk.

At the top of the first piece of paper there was the Navy submarine insignia. Then, under it, *U.S.S. SHARK*, Lieutenant Commander Paul Stevenson, U. S. Navy, Commanding.

The admiral read the pages slowly, finished them, and closed the folder. "Paul Stevenson shot from beyond thirty-five hundred yards," he said, frowning.

"Yes, sir."

"Why didn't he get in closer? He knew he was going to have to take a beating anyway. Why not make it worth while?"

"I don't think Paul has gotten—well, the feel of it yet, Admiral."

6

"Do you think he's a coward, Bill? If he is I want him out of the boats. Right *now*."

The commander hesitated. "Sir, Paul's boat isn't really on the ball yet. The crew doesn't seem to be with him yet——"

The admiral interrupted. "This didn't make the crew admire him—shooting from 'way out there. They must have thought he was scared to get in close and sink that ship."

"It might help to pull him and his crew together if he went on this special mission, Admiral. It won't be rough for the submarine, and it might give Paul a chance to get his feet under him. A chance to build up confidence in his crew."

"The *Shark's* going to make the trip but I'm not yet sure that Paul Stevenson is going to be her commanding officer," the admiral said. "A submarine is no place for a man who won't close the target. Who won't—fight."

"This special mission ought to tell the story one way or the other, Admiral. And, after all, it isn't like Mush Morton taking the *Wahoo* into the Sea of Japan. Paul can't get into anything too dangerous on the mission."

"No, I suppose not," the admiral agreed. "All right, let him go out on it. But if his boat doesn't come back here with all hands spoiling for a fight, he's through in the boats."

"He's outside now, Admiral. Do you want to talk to him?"

The admiral nodded.

In a moment, Paul Stevenson, commanding *Shark*, came into the room and closed the door. Paul was pale, thin, his mouth drawn tight and his eyes wary. He sat down in the chair and held his hands in his lap, his fingers wrapped tightly together.

"You had a lot of hard luck, Paul," the admiral said.

"Yes, sir, we did."

7

"On that second attack you shot from thirty-five hundred. That's pretty far out."

"We couldn't get in any closer, sir. He had destroyers patrolling all around him." The fingers began to move, gripping and regripping.

"They gave you a beating."

"Terrific, sir."

"Since you were going to get that hammering anyway, Paul, wouldn't you have felt better if you'd closed that tanker and nailed him?"

For a long time Stevenson sat there staring at the admiral. His eyes grew angry, white lines creased around the corners of his mouth. At last he said, "Do you mean I was afraid to close him?"

"Not afraid, Paul. Just not mad enough."

Stevenson stood up. "Admiral, you don't know what it's like out there. It's murder! *Murder.*"

The admiral said quietly, "I know it is, Paul." He pointed to the blackboard. Chalked on it were the words: OVERDUE AND PRESUMED LOST AS OF 1 JANUARY, 1943. Under that, the list of submarines: *Sealion*, S-36, S-26, *Perch*, S-27, S-39, *Grunion*, *Argonaut* . . . Name after name.

Stevenson said angrily, "You want me to put *Shark* on that list? You want me to close until they sink me?"

The admiral was still quiet, still friendly. "No, Paul. I want you to put *Shark* on the list with *Wahoo* and *Trigger* and *Tang*. I want to see your name up with Mush Morton, Red Ramage, and Donc Donaho."

"A guy gets lucky and it makes a hero out of him," Paul said.

"Or maybe he gets mad. He starts fighting." The admiral sat down on the desk. "Who's your Executive Officer, Paul?"

"Lieutenant Carney, sir."

"Good officer?"

Stevenson shrugged. "He's a reserve."

The admiral looked at him for a moment, and then said, "I've got a job for you, Paul. I'll tell you more about it later. Right now I want you to get *Shark* ready for sea."

"Right now, sir?"

The admiral nodded.

Stevenson waved his hands pitifully. "I've just come from sea, Admiral. We're whipped. We can't go out again right away."

"I'm not sending you into a hot zone, Paul. Just a cruise out to some islands and back again. No rough-stuff."

Stevenson walked slowly toward the admiral. "Sir, I know that we didn't sink a ship but we were out there for fifty-seven days. We need rest, sir."

The admiral looked at him. "Paul, the only other boat available for this job is *Wahoo*. She gets in today, and as soon as we can get some good torpedoes in her she's going back to the Sea of Japan."

"When do I have to go out, sir?"

"As soon as a j.g. makes up his mind," the admiral said.

CHAPTER 2

IT WAS MUCH HOTTER IN HAWAII than it had been in the States. Ken Braden could feel sweat soaking the starch out of his shirt as he walked slowly down the hill.

He had never seen so many things growing. All around him there were flowers, green grass, trees, bushes—everything green and growing and loaded with color. And the myna birds were everywhere, acting as though they owned the place.

Submarine.

There wasn't much green around Pearl Harbor itself. Mostly gray ships and black wharves and camouflaged dirty gray buildings. It looked messy down there, with bedding being aired on the ship's life lines, trucks and trains moving around, ships going in and out, and everywhere mountainous piles of gear, provisions, ammunition.

Submarine.

Ken caught up with a sailor and asked him where the submarines were based.

"Straight down the hill, sir."

He had never seen a submarine outside a newsreel but he had never liked the idea of them. Just thinking about it, he could feel the way it must be shut up inside one of them with the black, cold, silent water all around it and pressing in upon it. It would be like being trapped and helpless.

He went through an archway, showed his pass to the marine at the gate, and went on toward the open water of Pearl Harbor.

As he walked along he noticed that there wasn't much of the saluting and other military courtesies that they had had at the training school. Sailors overtook and passed him without any "By your leave, sir," and others went by without even glancing at him. Everyone seemed to be intent on something and in a hurry. Only he walked slowly, idly along.

Out on the submarine docks there was a good deal of moving around. A truck drove up and unloaded several sacks of mail, each one with a tag on it saying *U.S.S. Wahoo*. A group of high-ranking officers were talking beside a building. A gang of musicians, their instruments beside them, were sitting in the thin shade.

Only one submarine was tied up at the docks. Ken, remembering the admiral talking on the phone about *Wahoo* and *Shark*, decided that this must be the *Shark*. This was the submarine he would ride on—if he went out there.

Skirting the group of officers, he went along until he was beside the submarine.

She was old and ugly. The gray paint was peeling off, there was rust, almost red in the sunlight, on her. The long, low, narrow, flat fore- and afterdecks were cluttered with gear of all sorts and full garbage cans stood on the fantail.

She lay low in the dirty water and looked like something dead except that, from somewhere inside her, gouts of water were pulsing out of her as though she were breathing.

Ken stood for a long time looking at this boat. All of his horror at the idea of submarines came back strong.

There were only sailors on the deck, moving listlessly. Ken could hear no sound from inside her. She seemed, in her dirt and rust and ugliness, to have been abandoned by the Navy—like the battleships lying in the mud over by Ford Island.

But as Ken stood there a man at last came out of a

11

deck hatch and wandered toward the gangplank between the boat and the dock.

Ken would not have recognized him as a naval officer except for the tarnished brass bars of an ensign pinned to the unpressed, torn, faded khaki shirt.

The man had a black beard so long that it was hopelessly tangled. His officer's cap was crushed, the bill broken, the cover spotted with grease, the chin strap tarnished green. His shoes had rotted away in places so that his bare feet stuck through them.

This ensign walked listlessly to the gangway, pulled himself up, and went along the dock to a pair of bollards. He sat down on one, pushed his decrepit cap back on his head to let the sun shine on his pale gray face, and began to pull with his fingers at the knots in his beard.

Ken walked over and said, "Good morning."

The ensign gave him the sloppiest salute he had ever seen and said, "Good morning, Lieutenant."

"My name's Braden," Ken said.

"Malone."

Ken suddenly discovered that the ensign's eyes were bright blue and young. The beard was what made him look about fifty years old.

Over in the shade the musicians began to stir, picking up their instruments, playing single notes or little runs, the drummer tapping out a very soft beat. The group of officers also became more alert. A truck drove up with crates of milk and fruit so cold that the air condensed on them.

The ensign looked out over the harbor. "Wahoo's coming in," he announced.

Ken saw it now, too. The long, low, dark gray ship moving slowly and carefully toward the dock. It, too, was ugly with peeling paint and rust but it was shipshape and, somehow, far more lethal-looking than the submarine tied up in front of him.

"Man," the ensign said, "I'd love to be back in that boat."

Ken watched the *Wahoo* turn in toward the dock.

The ensign said, "I heard that the *Wahoo* got a load of faulty torpedoes. When she got out to the Sea of Japan with targets everywhere her fish wouldn't work. Boy, wouldn't that burn you! I bet the *Wahoo's* Old Man is *wild*."

The band began to play. Crews on the fore- and afterdecks of the *Wahoo* heaved lines ashore to the men on the dock and soon she was tied up.

Ken watched a lieutenant commander come down the conning tower ladder. Unlike Ensign Malone, the commander was shaved and clean, his cap military, his khakis almost as starched as Ken's own.

"That's Mush Morton," the ensign said. "Just the greatest submariner there ever was."

Morton saluted the group of officers, the band played, men hauled the mail and fruit aboard.

As Morton wheeled past Ken, with the officers hurrying to keep up with him, Ken saw his face.

Morton's face was almost white with anger. His eyes were blazing, his lips pressed together until they were gray. Both hands were clenched into fists, and as he walked he leaned forward like, Ken thought, a boxer going in.

As they passed, the bearded ensign said, "I told you Mush was mad. Did you see his face? Man, wouldn't that slay you—to take your boat right out under the gun, right into the Japoons back yard, and then have all your fish fail to fire?"

"Fish?"

The ensign looked bored. "Torpedoes, Lieutenant, torpedoes."

Ken said, "Oh," and sat down on the other bollard.

Morton had walked away so fast that the band was left playing by itself. The men of the *Wahoo* paid no attention to it as they settled down to eat fruit, drink milk, and read the mail. In a little while the music dribbled to a stop, the musicians packed up and left.

Ken had noticed that, in spite of what he had been taught during Navy indoctrination, submarines were referred to as "boats." He didn't want to get another "Torpedoes, Lieutenant," treatment, so he asked, "What's the name of your boat?"

Ensign Malone turned his head slowly, his beard flowing over his shoulder, and looked wearily at the submarine. Ken could see nothing but contempt in his eyes.

"That," the ensign said, "is the *So Scared Maru.* Wouldn't hurt a fly, that boat."

A marine on a motorcycle roared out on the dock and stopped in front of the ensign. Throwing a salute with machine precision, the marine pointed to the *Wahoo* and asked, "Is that the *Shark*, sir?"

The ensign gazed sorrowfully at the marine. "Son, don't let them hear you say that. That's the *Wahoo.*"

"I'm looking for the *Shark*, sir."

The ensign waved his hand wearily toward the submarine. "That is the *Shark.*"

"Where'll I find the Officer of the Deck? I've got a message for him."

"I am the Officer of the Deck."

The marine stared at him, surprised, but dug into the saddlebags and brought out an envelope. The ensign signed for it and the motorcycle roared away.

Ken waited until the ensign had read the message.

The ensign said, "Oh, the foulness of my fate," and stuffed the paper into his hip pocket. "We're going right back to sea. We have only spent fifty-seven days paddling around out there. We're tired, we're bushed, we're whipped, we don't like each other, we need a rest. But we're going right back to sea as soon as some j.g. makes up his mind about something." He turned and gazed

14

at Ken. "It must be wonderful to be a j.g., isn't it, Lieutenant?"

"Wonderful."

"I wouldn't be a j.g. for anything. Too much responsibility. . . . I wonder what this mysterious man is making up his mind about. I wonder where we're going. I wonder . . . I just wonder."

"It doesn't sound like you care much for submarines," Ken told him.

The ensign looked at the filthy, gray, rusty ship. Suddenly he was very serious. "You're wrong, Lieutenant. I like submarines. I wouldn't serve in anything else the Navy's got. But I'll tell you something, since you aren't in the boats and won't understand anyway, begging your pardon, Lieutenant, sir. I want to serve in a submarine that gets a band on the dock when she comes home. I want to serve in a submarine that comes home with a broomstick on her conning tower meaning she swept up her area, sank everything in sight, and shot all her fish. I want to serve in a submarine that goes in close and delivers. I want to serve in a submarine that when the cork comes down around your ears you don't mind so much because some Jap ship is going to the bottom with one of your fish in her belly. I want to serve in a submarine—— Say, how does it feel to be all shaved and iron-pants?"

"I've just come from the States," Ken apologized.

"The States? The United States of America? And how, pray, are they?"

"All right. What's it like in a submarine?"

"Depends on which one you're in." The ensign tried to get a finger through his beard so he could scratch. "I wonder if the *Wahoo* needs a real genius like me. Combination diving officer, navigator, torpedo mender, engineer, electrician, acey-deucy champ, and COM-SACKPAC. But nobody needs an ensign."

The ensign stood up, brushed off the seat of his already dirty trousers, saluted, and went back aboard the submarine. Ken could hear him yelling orders down the hatch, and soon a group of men, all with beards, came slowly out on deck. The ensign said something to them which started a violent argument.

The sun was setting now. Ken could see it through the window of his room in the Makapala Bachelor Officers' Quarters. The light grew soft over Pearl Harbor and began to fade on the great green mountains of Oahu.

Distances now seemed longer, and Ken thought again of those faraway enemy islands with the harsh, unfriendly names.

In the small room there were three double-decker bunks, six lockers, and some chairs. Five of the bunks had names on them, so he took the last one, a top bunk in the corner.

Sometime during the day his gear had come and was now in the middle of the room. There were two brandnew wooden crates and his Valpack.

The boxes were stencilled with his name and rank and nothing else. Then, instead of coming from the Supply Officer, Coronado, where the school was, they were marked Supply Officer, Mare Island.

Ken sat down in one of the chairs. The light faded away and left him, at last, in total darkness. The new, unpainted wood of the boxes gleamed a little and he could see the whiteness of the bedclothes, but the rest of the room was dark.

What should he do?

A feeling almost like anger stirred in him. How could they expect a man to say, "Yes, I'll risk my life," without even telling him what for—why? Without even telling him what they wanted him to do—or where—or how? How could he make a decision—with nothing?

Then he remembered the admiral's saying, "It's important. It'll save some lives, save some ships."

What did he have to do? What was going to threaten his life? Where would the submarine take him? What *was* the job?

The unanswered questions made him feel confused and helpless. Did he really *want* to risk his life?

Suddenly the lights snapped on and a full lieutenant came in, throwing his overseas cap on one of the beds. "Hello," he said, checking the blackout shields.

Ken, standing up at attention, said, "Good evening, sir."

"What's all this stuff?" the lieutenant asked, kicking one of the crates.

"Some gear of mine, sir."

The lieutenant stared at him. "How in the world can a j.g. accumulate that much gear? You must be going to war in a full-dress uniform complete with cocked hat and epaulets."

Ken, who was fairly sure what was in the crates, started to explain. Then he remembered the girl on Shell Beach, the man who had given him a lift. Embarrassed, he shoved the boxes out of the way as well as he could.

Soon four more lieutenants came in. After greeting Ken they ignored him and began talking among themselves. In a little while Ken guessed that they were communications officers, for they talked of NPM, FOX, decoding and dispatches.

One of them suddenly turned to Ken. "You must be fresh from Stateside."

"Fairly," Ken said.

"Are you a communicator?"

"No, sir. I'm just in the officers' pool."

"Oh. Then why were you assigned to this room?"

"I don't know, sir."

"Well, you might as well get squared away. You can

put your gear in that locker and we can get those crates out of here."

"I thought I'd just leave them unopened, sir, until I get assigned to a billet."

The lieutenant laughed. "That might be months from now. Anyway, no ship is going to let you lug that much stuff aboard. You might as well start getting rid of some of it now." He pulled open a drawer of the table and got a hammer. "Here," he said, tossing it.

Ken caught the hammer. Although he wasn't absolutely sure, he thought he knew what was in the crates. The masks, lungs, cylinders, and weights. He could hear the admiral saying, "I don't want anybody to know who you are . . . what your training has been. It may cost you your life."

But the lieutenant was looking at him, waiting for him to unpack.

Ken got up slowly and walked over to the crates. If he refused to open them it would be almost as bad as exposing the gear because the other officers would then get curious, or even suspicious. They might even *order* him to open them or, worse, get a lot of brass in here —Naval Intelligence people, security officers, and that sort of thing.

Ken hammered for a little while on one of the crates without getting any of the planks loose. Then suddenly he stared at his watch. Then he rushed for the door. "I'm supposed to be up at the submarine base right now. I almost forgot," he said, hurrying out.

He took the hammer with him.

Outside in the dark he walked fast until he could no longer see the BOQ. Then he slowed down.

He walked until after midnight. When he got back to the room there was no light, and as he silently went in he could hear the other officers in their beds.

The crates were where he had left them, still closed.

18

Undressing in the dark, he climbed up to his bunk and lay down.

But he couldn't think. Lying there with his hands under his head, he simply could not think. The room was full of the sounds of men breathing and snoring and moving.

Why had he been picked for this job? He was only one of tens of thousands of people in the Navy; just another j.g. Another civilian dressed up in a sailor suit; another reserve officer like the five sleeping around him.

Those five weren't going out, alone, to risk their lives. They were going, every day, up the hill to CINCPAC to code and decode messages.

Although he had no idea what it was the admiral wanted him to do, he could at least guess that it had to do with something under water. Why else would they have asked for volunteers from the UDT school? Maybe it was blowing mines on a Jap beach, or planting them; maybe it was just to do a recon on a beach or an island. But, whatever it was, it was dangerous.

He wasn't a very good swimmer. There'd been plenty in his class who were better. And he hadn't done too well during Hell Week when they had tried to find out who was physically capable of taking the punishment of underwater training and who wasn't. He'd barely endured that long week of physical and mental torture.

Why should he risk his life?

At last, he went to sleep.

Sometime before dawn he woke up again. The communicators were still breathing and snoring, the double-decker beds creaking as they moved.

Outside there was a full, warm moon and some sort of night birds were singing.

Ken wondered suddenly what the moon looked like tonight to the men in the prison camps of Japan. He wondered if night birds were singing out there, too.

Suddenly, and for no reason, Ken thought about the ensign with the dirty beard and rotten shoes and greasy cap.

"I want to serve . . ."

CHAPTER 3

AT THE UNDERWATER DEMOLITION SCHOOL reveille had been at six in the morning. Now, in Pearl Harbor, Ken woke up on the dot of six. The communicators were still snoring but the myna birds were awake and endlessly fighting.

He got dressed quickly and quietly. In the mess hall there were only a few officers having breakfast.

At the sub base there was already a commotion around the *Shark*. Trucks were drawn up alongside and lines of men were handing down provisions and supplies. Torpedoes were being loaded into her through hatches in the decks and men were passing ammunition for the 5-inch guns.

He had not realized how big the torpedoes were. He guessed that they were twenty feet long and, from the way the men were working, must weigh a ton.

He found Ensign Malone directing the torpedo loading through the forward hatch. His cap was just as battered and greasy, but he had washed his beard so that it now shone black, thick, and curly in the sunlight.

"Good morning, Lieutenant Braden," Malone said, going through the sloppy salute.

"Morning, Mr. Malone," Ken said, returning it.

Malone directed a crew handling a diesel fuel hose line and, after he had it placed where he wanted it, came over to stand by Ken.

"Hope that j.g. has a hard time making up his mind, I'd like to get a day off. If I had a day off, do you know what I'd do?"

21

"Shave?"

"I'd shave if I had *two* days off. But not for just one. No, I'd get five gallons of milk and go lie on the beach. I'd lie there all day long without thinking. I'm tired of thinking, Lieutenant."

"What do you think about so hard?"

"Mostly about what I'd do if I was Skipper of this boat. The first thing I'd do, I'd pass a law. Now hear this, there will be no torpedo shooting beyond a range of fifteen hundred yards. Then I'd pass another law. The *U.S.S. Shark* will not withdraw from the scene of battle just because there are too many enemy ships around or because they're too big. I would soon be known throughout the fleet as Menace Malone. But, since I've got to get myself promoted all the way from ensign to commander, I doubt if those laws ever get passed aboard this scow. So I will continue to be known as Mixed-up Malone."

A chief petty officer came over and said, "All torpedoes aboard, sir."

"All good fish and true, Chief?" Malone asked.

"That I wouldn't know. I was talking to *Wahoo's* Chief of the Boat last night. They had a foul time out there. Plenty of targets, targets everywhere, and just one faulty fish after the other. Every time they fired the roof fell in. Once the Jap cans dropped stuff on them for thirty hours straight. He says Captain Morton is ready to go to Washington and blow up the Bureau of Ordnance."

"I'll go with him," Malone said.

The chief said, "These fish we've got are a new type. The boys guarantee 'em. When are we shoving off, sir?"

Malone shrugged. "Our fate lies in the hands of a j.g. We shove off when he makes up his mind."

"Oh no!" the chief said. "What is this, a special mission of some sort?"

"I don't know. But it sure looks like it."

The chief said, walking away, "That this should happen to us."

"He doesn't seem to be very happy," Ken remarked.

"He isn't. None of us are. This is not a happy ship, Lieutenant."

A clock somewhere began to strike and Malone said, "Colors."

Ken, also standing at attention and saluting the flag, glanced at Malone out of the corner of his eye. In spite of the greasy cap and the beard, the rotten shoes and torn clothing, Malone seemed military. There was something about him—a strength and a purpose that you could see now, and feel.

At the end Malone said, "Eight bells and I'm still an ensign. Well, so long, Lieutenant, sir. With your permission, I'll be shoving off to continue my many duties both above and below."

Ken turned away from the *Shark* and started up the hill.

The sun now was hot, so he walked slowly, trying not to sweat.

In the admiral's outer office the commander greeted him and called the admiral on the squawk box. "Ask him to come in," the admiral's voice answered.

Ken went into the now familiar room and closed the door.

"Sit down, Braden. Don't they have wonderful mornings out here in Hawaii?"

Ken glanced out the window. "Yes, sir . . . I've made up my mind, sir."

The admiral waited a moment, looking at him. "Yes? Or no?"

"Yes," Ken said.

"Are you sure?" the admiral asked quietly.

Ken nodded.

The admiral said slowly, "You know that you may not come back, don't you?"

"Yes, sir."

The admiral stood for a long time looking out the

window. At last, with a quick movement, he turned, picked an envelope off his desk, and held it out. "All right, Braden, here are your orders. As soon as *Shark* is ready for sea I'll come down and give you more details. Since you'll be leaving very soon, I advise you to write home. But, please, leave your letters with the commander here for censoring." Then, although his voice was still pleasant, he added, "Nothing else you write will ever leave this island."

"Aye, aye, sir."

"And here," the admiral went on, "are some Japanese language books and a dictionary with a special list of Jap ideographs for time, location, places, ship types, movement, and geography. Bone up on them; I'll tell you why later."

"Aye, aye, sir."

The admiral shook hands without saying anything.

Ken went back out into the blazing sunshine and walked down the hill to the sub base. Around the *Shark* there were now even more trucks. Ken hunted out Malone. "I'm reporting aboard for transportation," he said, showing him the orders.

Malone glanced at them. "Oh, so you're the mysterious j.g. controlling my pitiful fate. Where're we going? What we gonna do? Maybe capture Tokyo Rose, hunh?"

"I don't know," Ken said.

"They tell me she's a dish."

"Never heard of the gal," Ken admitted.

Malone glanced at him. "You will," he said quietly. "Well, come aboard. Let's see if we can find the captain."

"You lead the way, will you?" Ken asked. "I don't know anything about submarines."

"The blind leading the blind," Malone said, jumping over on the *Shark's* deck.

Ken, feeling clumsy and in the way, followed through the working parties, narrowly escaping being knocked into the water by a crate in a sling.

They climbed a steel ladder going up to the surprisingly small, cramped bridge of the boat, and then Malone disappeared down a hatch.

Ken followed, barking his shins on the sharp edge of the deck.

It was almost like climbing down into a can full of fishing worms. As far as Ken could tell, there was no open space anywhere. There was nothing but machinery; controls, valves, handles, wheels, dials, levers, lights, pipes, wires, tubes, switches, engines, motors, bells, horns, batteries, boxes. Moving in and around and through all this were men, so that it was hard to get anywhere.

The thing that surprised Ken the most, however, was the *brightness*. After seeing the dull, dirty, rusty outside of the boat he had not expected to find this blazing light, this spotlessly clean, shining interior. Everything was painted or varnished or polished so that it sparkled.

Going down through another hatch, Malone at last turned and wormed his way along past men carrying meat, vegetables, pieces of machinery, belts of ammunition, boxes, tools, or past men working on things.

They ducked through a vertical hatch and came out into a narrow passageway with, on both sides, tiny rooms filled from deck to overhead with built-in metal bunks.

At last Malone stopped at one of the rooms with a gray curtain for a door. He knocked and a voice answered, "Come in."

This was the only room having just one bed. It wasn't any bigger than a closet, but it had a small desk, the bed, and a washbasin which folded back against the wall.

A lieutenant commander was sitting at the desk studying some papers. For a moment he didn't look up as Malone pulled the curtain aside.

25

Ken could see that the commander was angry about something.

Malone said, "Captain Stevenson, here's our passenger."

"Very well," the commander said, not looking up.

Malone made a gesture of farewell to Ken and went on down the corridor.

Ken, waiting, pressed himself against the wall so that people could get by. He wished that the commander would at least ask him to come in so that he could get out of the way but, for some minutes he went on studying the papers.

A man in dungarees with a beard almost as huge as Malone's came by carrying a box which knocked Ken's papers out of his hand. Before he could pick them up another man kicked them down the corridor and stepped on them.

Ken was scrambling around, picking up the papers, when the commander at last said, "Well, let's see your orders."

Ken handed him the papers, which were now covered with the print of a big, oily foot.

"I can't read through all this gook," the commander complained.

"They order me to report to you for transportation, sir," Ken told him.

"What do they think this is, the *Queen Mary?*" He looked at Ken's orders. "I can't even read your name."

"Braden, sir. Kenneth M."

"Very well. What's this mission all about?"

Ken had assumed that the admiral would have told him. This must be, he decided, another test. "I don't know, sir."

The commander seemed outraged. "*Mister* Braden! In the Navy you don't say, 'I don't know.' Now what's this mission all about?"

Ken had heard of these hard-rock skippers but this was the first one he'd run into. Trying to control his own anger, he said, "The admiral said he would come down just before we go to sea and give us some details, sir. I imagine he'll explain then what the mission is all about."

"You certainly do imagine a great deal, Lieutenant. Very well. Shove off."

Ken hesitated, then said, "Sir, I've got some gear."

"Have you?" the commander asked, not looking up.

"Yes, sir. It's fairly heavy, sir."

"Well, what are you going to do about it?"

"I'd like to get it aboard, sir."

The commander looked wearily up at him. "Do you want me to bring it down here piggy-back, Lieutenant?"

Ken could feel the blood hot in his face. "No, sir. I thought perhaps I could borrow a jeep or something."

"Submarines are not equipped with jeeps or something."

Ken gave up. Saluting, he turned.

Trying to get out of the boat, he lost his way. He found a vertical hatch identical to the one Malone had led him through and climbed into a compartment as full of working men as the rest of them. Making his way slowly, he eased past some pipe berths, machinery and valves, went down a short flight of steps, and came at last to a solid wall covered with gadgets, pipes, dials, wires, and tubes.

Turning around, he asked a bearded sailor in nothing but shorts how to get out.

"Not that way," the man said. "Unless you want to go out through the torpedo tube."

Ken at last got back on the dock. He felt as though he had just come through a football scrimmage—and he wasn't playing on either team.

As his anger at the submarine's commander died a

wave of depression and fear swept over him. He had never in his life felt so completely alone, completely left out of everything.

CHAPTER 4

ENSIGN MALONE HAD STRIPPED to the waist and was helping a chief petty officer rig the forward gun for sea. When he saw Ken come up out of the boat and walk dejectedly over to the dock, he stopped working for a moment and watched him. "Take over, will you, Chief. We've got trouble," Malone said quietly. Then he jumped over to the dock.

"How'd you make out with the Skipper?" he asked.

"Not very well."

"Too bad. Maybe he's just bushed after fifty-seven days at sea. That's a long time in a submarine."

"So is five minutes," Ken said. "Look, I've got to get some gear aboard. Is there any chance of getting some transportation for it?"

"How much gear you got?"

Ken measured off the size of the crates with his arms. Malone looked horrified. "Where can we put them? Oh well, me for the jolly sailor's life. Let's see if we can beat somebody out of a jeep."

The best they could do was a weapons carrier, which Malone drove over to BOQ. When he saw the two crates he stared. "Son—I mean, Lieutenant, sir—we can't get things that size in the *Shark*. They're bigger'n Grant's Tomb. Can't you unpack them and get them so we can stow the pieces?"

Ken shook his head.

"Spy stuff, eh?" Malone asked quietly.

"Something like that."

Still grumbling, Malone helped him load them into

the carrier then unload them and get them down through the *Shark's* forward hatch.

Down in the boat Malone and Ken looked at the crates cluttering up the forward torpedo room. In the submarine they looked even bigger and more awkward.

Behind them a voice snapped, "Attention!"

Malone and Ken turned. Coming through the hatch were Stevenson and another officer. Stevenson walked up to Ken's crates and said, "May I ask what this hurrah's nest is doing here?"

No one answered so he turned to Malone. "What's in these boxes, Mr. Malone?"

"I don't know, sir," Malone told him.

"In the Navy we don't say, 'I don't know,' Mr. Malone. We say, 'I'll find out.'"

Ken said, "Captain, that's my gear, sir."

The commander stared at him. "Yours? What do you think this boat is, a transatlantic liner? Get this stuff out of the boat."

"I'll need it, sir," Ken said.

Stevenson said coldly, "Officers in my ship are allowed to stow only sufficient work and dress uniforms for a war patrol, toilet articles, stationery, and necessary professional books."

Then he turned to Malone. "Get these crates up on the dock and open them. You can then advise Mr. Braden as to what clothing he will need. Since he is a passenger I want his gear kept to an absolute minimum. Do you understand?"

"Aye, aye, sir."

Ken knew that to unpack the crates on the dock where there were all sorts of civilians as well as military people would tell a simple story—the submarine was taking an Underwater Demolition man somewhere. The admiral wouldn't like that.

On the other hand, the commander had a right to order the stuff out of his boat.

Ken had felt from the first that Stevenson didn't like him; that he blamed him for having to go to sea again so soon; that he considered him, at least, a nuisance.

None of this would help him, Ken knew. And to have the commanding officer's enmity might even hurt him—hurt him enough to make his job harder, make it impossible.

"May I talk to you alone, sir?" Ken asked.

"What for?" the commander asked. "There aren't any secrets on my boat, Lieutenant."

"This isn't a secret, sir, I'd just like to talk with you alone."

"Oh, very well," Stevenson said. "In the meantime, Mr. Malone, get this junk out of here and opened up on the dock."

"Would it be all right to leave it here until we finish talking, sir?" Ken asked.

Stevenson seemed to be extremely annoyed. "Mr. Braden, has it occurred to you that I, and not you, am the commanding officer of this ship?"

"I'm sorry, sir. But could I talk to you for just a minute?"

Stevenson wheeled and marched aft. Before Ken followed him he whispered fast to Malone, "Leave that stuff alone. Don't open it, *please.*"

Stevenson had gone back to his cabin. Ken knocked and pushed the curtain aside.

"All right, what is it?" Stevenson snapped at him.

"Sir, what's in those crates is necessary to the mission," Ken told him. "But the admiral doesn't want anyone to know what it is until we're at sea."

"What is this mysterious gear, Mr. Braden?"

"I don't know, sir."

The commander put both hands over his face. " 'I don't know! I don't know!' That's all I hear since the reserves joined the Navy." He started to say something else but a dark-haired, serious-looking officer knocked and pushed the curtain aside. "Boat's ready for sea, sir. Except for some crates in the forward torpedo room which haven't been stored."

Stevenson said, "They belong to our dashing young hero. Leave 'em where they are."

"In a seaway they might shift and do some damage, Captain," the lieutenant said.

Stevenson didn't even look at him. "I said leave 'em." Then he reached for the phone. In a moment he said, "This is the commanding officer of the *Shark* reporting ready for sea. Yes, sir. Aye, aye, sir."

He hung up and looked at the serious lieutenant. "The admiral will be aboard in five minutes. Have the crew stand by, he may inspect the boat."

The lieutenant saluted and left.

Stevenson said, "You are to wait in the wardroom, Mr. Braden."

"Yes, sir. Where is it, sir?"

"Right behind you, Mr. Braden."

Ken walked across the corridor into a tiny, well-lighted room. A table covered with a green cloth almost completely filled it, so that he had to slide sideways to get around to a built-in seat on the outboard side. On the walls there were racks with technical books, a complicated-looking radio, and various dials and gauges. In the wall at one end of the tiny room there was an opening through which he could see a kitchen so small he wondered how anyone could get into it to cook.

It didn't take the admiral long to get down there. He and Stevenson came into the wardroom. The admiral tossed a sealed envelope on the table. Ken saw that it had only the single word SCAN on it.

The admiral waited for Stevenson to pull the curtains across the entrances to the room, then he sat down. "Is your gear aboard, Braden?"

"Yes, sir."

"Have you opened it?"

"No, sir."

"Good. . . . Now, Paul," he said, turning to Stevenson, "we've got an unusual setup here, but this is turning out to be an unusual war. Now none of what I'm going to tell you is on paper. We don't want any information leaks. So let's keep all this between the three of us."

Lying on the green cloth of the table was a Coca-Cola bottle cap. Stevenson frowned toward the galley as the admiral picked it up.

"Here's Pearl Harbor," the admiral said, putting the bottle cap down in the center of the table. "The war plans room." Then he put a pencil down at the edge of the table. "And here's Japan—Tokyo. About three thousand miles away."

He touched the bottle cap. "All right, here in the war plans room Admiral Nimitz and his staff discuss how they can stop the Japanese march across the Pacific and, once it's stopped, how to slam them back to here." He touched the pencil. "Those discussions are absolutely top secret and known only to a few men.

"And yet," the admiral said, "what was said in the war plans room was reaching Tokyo in a few days, sometimes within a few hours." The admiral looked first at Ken and then at Stevenson. "You see, we had a traitor in there. A man who was costing us the lives of ships and men. We still have him but—now—we know who he is."

The admiral got a penny out of his pocket and put it down close to the bottle cap. "Here's a radio transmitter. It's run by Japanese spies and is somewhere in the Hawaiian Islands. Our traitor feeds it information which it sends out. This transmitter is using a code which we've broken and can read. From here"—he tapped the penny—"our secrets are being beamed straight across the Pacific. But—and this is where you, Paul, and Braden come into the picture—this transmitter is not capable of getting its messages all the way to Tokyo. Our electronics people figure that it has a maximum range of two thousand miles, which leaves it a thousand miles short."

The admiral put a twenty-five-cent piece down halfway between the bottle cap and the pencil. "Here's what happens. Within an hour or so after the transmitter in Hawaii finishes a message another transmitter out in the middle of the Pacific—here—opens up. We've had a submarine out there for weeks now and this mid-Pacific transmitter never broadcasts until after the one in Hawaii does.

"The trouble is that this baby"—he tapped the twenty-five-cent piece—"uses a different code. The cryptanalysts have about given up on it and doubt if it can be broken in under six months. That's too long, gentlemen."

The admiral stopped and looked at Ken. Quietly he said, "We want you to go get that code."

Ken looked at the twenty-five-cent piece and then at the admiral. There wasn't anything to say.

Stevenson spoke for the first time. "Admiral, wouldn't it be a lot easier to concentrate on this spy transmitter in Hawaii? Just eliminate that and the whole network collapses. Put some radio direction finders on him, nail him down from three points, then go in and knock him off."

"That's one way, Paul. But we don't *want* the network destroyed. We want to use this setup ourselves—from traitor to Tokyo. Only from now on the information he gets will be information we want him to have. In order to do that we've got to know two things: where is this transmitter?" He touched the twenty-five-cent piece. "We believe it's on an island rather than in a ship or submarine. But we'd like to know exactly so we can put a monitor on him and be sure he's sending along the information we want him to send. Then, number two, we've got to have his code so we can read him. Once

34

we know that we can go ahead with the second phase of the plan.

"What we're doing is this: although he doesn't know it, the traitor has already been isolated completely. He still sits in on planning sessions, as usual, but the war plans discussed with him are not our real plans. They are similar enough in detail so that he won't get suspicious but they are not only useless to Tokyo but will, we hope, trick units of the Jap Navy into positions where we can knock them off."

The admiral picked up the bottle cap, the penny, and the pencil, but left the twenty-five-cent piece lying on the green cloth. Then, turning to Ken, he said, "It's up to you, Ken. I can't even help you with the details because we don't know any more about this transmitter setup than you do. You'll just have to work it out when you get there. One more thing, the Japs on that island must never even suspect that we know they're there. If they do they'll change codes or move somewhere else. You must not be caught, Ken, nor even seen."

Ken nodded but didn't say anything.

The admiral turned to Stevenson. "I don't want you going on the prod, Paul. Don't hunt for trouble. But, if it comes—fight. The important thing, of course, is to get Braden to the islands and—get him back."

"I'll see to that, sir," Stevenson said.

"Good. Now on the voyage out, Ken, study that Japanese dictionary so that you'll be able to recognize a code if you see one. Now, Paul, here are your charts. We think the transmitter is on one of these six islands. But if it isn't take a look at this group down here."

"Aye, aye, sir."

The admiral picked up the twenty-five cents and stood up. "All right, that's it."

Stevenson and Ken stood up, and Stevenson asked, "How much of this can I tell the crew, sir?"

The admiral hesitated. "Not much, Paul. I want no

talk about the leak in Pearl, or about transmitters. None of that. Tell them you're scouting the islands for possible invasion points."

"Aye, aye, sir."

The admiral held out his hand to Ken. "Good luck. The very *best*."

"Good-by, sir."

The admiral turned then to Stevenson. "Paul, let's have a look at these new cabins for sub skippers I hear BuShips is turning out."

In Stevenson's cabin the admiral pulled the heavy curtain across the door and faced Stevenson. "What do you know about this underwater stuff, Paul? These diving rigs they've got now, and all that?"

"Well, sir, it's all pretty new and I've been at sea for the last fifty-seven days, you know."

The admiral nodded. "I don't know much about it either. So we'll just have to leave that phase of it up to Braden. He's fresh out of UDT and should know what he's doing."

Stevenson's usually pale, grayish face began to turn a faint pink with anger. "Do you mean, sir, that I'm to take orders from a j.g.?"

"Certainly not, Paul. I mean only that he'll need all the co-operation you can give him. He'll need maneuvers, dives, ways of getting in and out of the boat, rendezvous, which you'll have to let him have. In that connection I want you to take—any—risk—you feel is justified, Paul."

Stevenson's face was still pale pink as he said, "Aye, aye, sir."

The admiral sat down on the bed. "You're not very happy about this, are you, Paul?"

"It's not a question of happiness, sir. But I don't see how they can expect one man, especially a j.g. right out of civilian life, to go out there and get that code.

Why don't they send a Marine raiding party out there and take over that island?"

The admiral said patiently, "We don't want that island, Paul. We only want the code."

Stevenson fiddled with the gold eagle on his cap as he said, slowly, "Well, Admiral, I think they've picked the wrong man for the job. Braden may be able to swim like a fish but—in my opinion—he hasn't got what it takes. In the first place, he won't obey orders. I ordered him to get some crates out of the boat and he stood there and argued with me. He doesn't know the first thing about discipline."

The admiral hid the strong doubt now running through his mind as he said, "Maybe not. But he was hand-picked for this job so you'll just have to put up with his civilian ways."

"Yes, sir. I understand that, sir. But, from what I've seen of him, I just wonder if he's got the guts it's going to take to do this thing."

The admiral said slowly, "So do I, Paul. I don't think I've got enough guts even to try it, but maybe he has."

"Why didn't they pick a real Navy man then instead of one of these ninety-day wonders?"

"I don't think the Regular Navy has any corner on guts, Paul. Some men have 'em, some don't." The admiral stood up. "Good-by, and good luck," he said. "Do the best you can, Paul."

PART II—UP PERISCOPE!

CHAPTER 1

ENSIGN MALONE PUSHED THE CURTAIN aside and stood back. "Welcome to my mansion, Lieutenant," he said, bowing. "This, sir, is our home away from home."

Ken looked in. The room was no bigger than a closet. Three built-in bunks covered the entire far wall. Another wall was covered with small lockers while the third had a medicine chest and Pullman-type washbasin. There were no chairs, no tables, there was no space.

Ensign Malone peered in over Ken's shoulder. "I think there's something you ought to know, Lieutenant, sir," he said. "In order to live in this vast amount of space only one of us can take a breath at a time. You'll soon get used to it."

"How many people live in here?" Ken asked.

"Only three of us," Malone told him. "The bottom bunk is the sole property of one Lieutenant (j.g.) Silas Mount. The next one is—well, er, sir—mine. Unless, of course, you are impolite enough to pull your great rank and order me out of it. Otherwise, the top one will be yours. You are most fortunate, Lieutenant, because the man in the top bunk enjoys many privileges, including stepping on everybody else when getting in or out of his sack. The top bunk is also not where we all sit.

We sit on the bottom bunk regardless of whether anyone is in it."

Malone was about to say something else when the diesels started. "Oh-oh. Here we go. Down in the wild blue yonder."

"Are we leaving?"

Malone nodded.

"I think I'll go topside and see the sights. This is the first time I've ever been on a sub."

Malone glanced over at him. "I'd stay down here, Lieutenant," he said seriously. "The Skipper's sort of particular about people on the bridge. Especially when he's maneuvering. If you haven't got a job up there you'd better stay below."

Ken thanked him and went into the tiny room. Malone disappeared down the corridor.

There was no place to sit in the room except on the beds, so Ken climbed up to the top bunk and sat down, his feet hanging down almost to the bunk below.

He could hear faintly the commands from the bridge. "Take in four." The diesels, idling, filled the ship with a low, panting hum.

The voice drifted down, "Take in one. All back full."

The diesels stepped up their panting and Ken felt the ship heave itself backward.

He pulled his feet up and stretched out on the bunk. "Ahead one third, left full rudder."

The ship slowed, stopped, went forward. In the harbor there was no wave motion, so it was hard for him to tell that the ship was moving. Soon, though, as the *Shark* passed out through the opening in the anti-submarine net at the entrance to Pearl Harbor, she was in the waves of the open sea. Now she rolled a little and Ken could hear the sound of water slapping against the steel hull.

He wondered if he would ever come back into that calm, deep, scarred harbor.

Malone stuck his head into the room and grinned when he saw Ken lying in his bunk. "You'll make a good submariner, Lieutenant. The first law of the sea is to sack out. The Skipper wants to see you in his cabin."

"Thanks." Ken swung his legs over and climbed down.

At the captain's cabin he knocked and went in. Stevenson was sitting at the desk reading some papers. He kept on reading as Ken stood at attention in the doorway.

At last Stevenson glanced up at him. "Don't just stand there. Come in and pull the curtain."

"Aye, aye, sir."

There was nowhere to sit except the captain's bed so Ken remained at attention.

"Well," Stevenson said, "have you gone over the op plan?"

Ken didn't know what an "op plan" was so he shook his head.

"Well, what have you been doing?"

"Nothing, sir."

Stevenson sighed loudly and swung around in the chair. "That's a good beginning. That impresses me, Mr. Braden. You must be a very brave young man to be going out on an assignment like this without even studying the op plan." He reached into the desk and got out the envelope marked SCAN. "I'm quite sure that the admiral went to a lot of trouble to work up this op plan. He'd be hurt if he knew that you just aren't interested in it."

Ken started to point out to Stevenson that he couldn't very well study the "op plan" as long as it was locked in Stevenson's desk, but he changed his mind and said nothing.

"Have you gotten those crates out of the way yet?"

"No, sir."

"Why not?"

"I don't know where to stow the gear, sir."

Stevenson sighed again, loudly. "Stow it in your cabin, Mr. Braden." Then he swung all the way around so that he was facing Ken. "Since you're not interested in the op plan, perhaps I can interest you in a few other things."

Ken, still standing at attention, looked steadily at Stevenson's pale, gray face with the dishwater blue eyes.

"In the first place," Stevenson said, "there are eight officers and seventy-four men in this boat—not counting you. Do you know who is responsible for keeping these officers and men alive?"

"You, sir?"

"Right! Check! That's my first duty, and I want you to keep it firmly in mind, Mr. Braden. I make the decisions in this boat—*all* of them."

"Yes, sir." Ken wondered why Stevenson was giving him this lecture. He also wondered about the things he had studied in the Regulations for governing the Navy. He couldn't remember the Regulations saying anything about the commanding officer's first duty being to keep his men alive. It seemed to Ken that one of the first duties of a commanding officer was to engage the enemy and fight.

"Now—if you can spare the time, Mr. Braden—I'd like for you to take this op plan and study it. Then, when you think you understand it, I want you to give me an operation plan of your own. This must include what you intend to do and how you intend to do it. With all the details. In writing. But—keep in mind as you make your plans that I and not you, am Skipper of this boat. I, and not you, will decide whether what you plan to do can be done. Is that clear?"

"Yes, sir."

"But—first—get that gear out of my torpedo room."

"Aye, aye, sir."

"That's all, Mr. Braden."

Ken hesitated. "May I have the op plan, sir?"

Stevenson looked at him for a long time. "What was my first order to you, Mr. Braden?"

"To study the op plan and make a report, sir."

"Wrong," Stevenson said coldly. "That was a request. My first *order* was to get that junk out of my torpedo room."

"Yes, sir."

"Not 'Yes, sir,' Mr. Braden. 'Aye, aye, sir.' That means to a naval officer 'I understand and *will* obey.' 'Yes, sir,' means nothing."

"Yes, sir."

Stevenson sighed loudly again and turned back to his desk.

Ken walked slowly back to his cabin. As his anger at Stevenson subsided, in its place came the knowledge that he was in serious trouble. Without Stevenson's help he didn't see how he could do his job.

Ken went on to the forward torpedo room. It was filled with men stowing gear in the small lockers or lying in the tiers of pipe berths which hung on both sides of the room. Behind the berths Ken could see the oiled bodies of torpedoes.

As he was asking a chief petty officer for a hammer and screwdriver, Malone, his beard still clean and shiny, stepped through the low hatch. "Ahhh," he said. "Santa Claus is now going to open his sackful of presents."

Ken ripped open the first of the crates. "The Skipper says for me to stow this stuff in our cabin," he informed Malone.

"Oh no!" Malone cried. "It can't be done. There's no room for it."

Ken shrugged. "Where, then?"

"What is the stuff?"

Ken lifted back the wooden top. In this crate there were only air and oxygen cylinders and cans of soda lime for the rebreather. In the other crate there were the face masks and tubes for the rebreathers and two plain face masks. The knife, wrist compass, watches, rubber suits, fins, and gauges were packed separately. There were also two tiny Minox cameras in waterproof cases. In addition there was a complicated-looking valve with a book of instructions.

Ken unpacked the stuff as members of the crew stood around and watched. Suddenly he wondered if he could get oxygen and air on the sub. Turning to Malone, he asked about it.

"How much oxygen have we got, Chief?" Malone asked the Chief of the Boat, a lean, muscular, handsome petty officer still wearing a complete uniform.

"Full up, Mr. Malone."

Malone turned to Ken. "How much will you need?"

Ken picked up one of the oxygen bottles. "A bottle will last me from two to two and a half hours under water," he said. "It just depends on how scared I get."

Malone looked puzzled and Ken grinned. "The scareder you are the faster you breathe and the more oxygen you use." Then he asked about air. "Is there any way we can compress pure air down to around two thousand pounds per square inch?"

The Chief of the Boat laughed. "If you want, we'll squeeze it down to three thousand psi, sir."

"That'd be even better," Ken said.

The Chief of the Boat said, "At two hours per bottle we can keep the lieutenant under water for about a year."

Malone laughed and asked if the chief could stow any of the gear.

"I can take care of the bottles in the racks, sir. I don't know about all these tubes and things, though."

Malone looked morosely at the diving gear. "Oh well, outranked again. I'll give you half my locker space, which will leave me just enough room to stow my toothbrush."

As Ken and Malone gathered up the gear the chief

asked, "Is the Skipper going to give us the word about where we're going, Mr. Malone?"

Malone looked at Ken. "I think so," Ken said.

The chief looked steadily at him. "We'd like to know, Lieutenant. We'd sort of like to know why we have to go out again without any rest after a fifty-seven-day patrol."

"I don't blame you, Chief," Ken told him, "but it isn't my job to give you the word."

"No, I guess not," the chief agreed. "I hope the Skipper doesn't forget to tell us."

Back in Malone's cabin they somehow managed to get the gear stowed so that the three officers could, at least, get into their beds and stand up in front of the washbasin.

With that done Ken went back to Stevenson's cabin. "The gear is stowed, sir. May I have the op plan now?"

"Mr. Braden," Stevenson said, "will you please allow me to decide whether the gear is stowed properly or not?"

Stevenson marched forward to the torpedo room. Some men were knocking the crates apart and getting them ready to heave overboard after nightfall.

Stevenson inspected the stowage of the air and oxygen bottles and then came aft to inspect Ken's cabin. Some of the tubes were still visible and the face masks hung on clothing hooks on the bulkhead. "Is that the best you can do, Mr. Braden?" he demanded.

"I think it is, sir."

"Do you realize how much of an inconvenience all this junk is to the working officers who have to live in here? I don't suppose you do." Stevenson whirled around and went on to his own cabin.

"All right, Mr. Braden," he said, handing Ken the SCAN envelope. "I want your op plan by twenty hundred tonight."

"Aye, aye, sir."

44

Stevenson almost smiled. "That's better."

In the corridor Ken glanced at his watch. Eleven-thirty. He had eight and a half hours.

Back in his cabin he climbed up and settled down in his bunk. Opening the envelope, he first studied the chart. The six islands the admiral had pointed out formed a huge atoll, the islands scattered around the lagoon in a rough circle. Their real names had been taken off the chart and code names put on. The biggest of the islands had been named Sunset, then there were Sunrise, Dawn, Noon, Midnight, and Morning.

He had just begun to think about the whole situation as a series of problems when Malone came in.

"Ahhh," Malone said, seeing the charts and papers. "The—secret papers. Where we going, Lieutenant, sir? What we gonna get done to us when we get there?"

"I wish I knew," Ken told him. "Haven't had time to find out yet. What's the boat doing?"

"Well, Lieutenant, sir, we're steaming peacefully along at eighteen knots in the general direction of Midway Island. If our Executive Officer, Lieutenant Carney, knows anything about navigation—which he do—we will find the island of Midway and will thereupon refuel and be on our merry way."

"Are we above the water or below it?" Ken asked.

"Good question. But I will let you in on a little sub-mariner's secret. When you hear an old-fashioned auto-mobile horn go 'Aaah—ooogah, aaah—ooogah' you will know that we are preparing to get ready to see if we can make this boat go down under the water."

"What does it feel like when you get under there?"

"Hah!" Malone exclaimed with joy. "Now's my chance to explain the horrors of the deep, the ghastly shut-in feeling, the clammy darkness of the dreadful abyss. Let me tell you, Lieutenant, just what it feels like to be below the surface in a submarine. It feels like—nothing at all, just rides smoother. If it weren't for the horn and

45

a certain amount of activity you wouldn't even know you were under water. That is—ordinarily."

Ken grinned. "So what's it like when it isn't—ordinarily?"

Malone's expression changed. "There's no describing that. When the heat's up to a hundred and twenty and the air's so foul you can slice it with a knife. When there's water coming into the boat and the depth charges are coming down on it. Well, that's a different thing."

"Have you been depth-charged?"

"Not in this boat. Not seriously, anyway. But I took one working over in *Wahoo* before I was transferred here."

"Tell me about it," Ken asked.

Malone grinned. "There's no way to tell you about it. If you've never been through it you can't understand how it feels. It's like nothing else in the world."

"Bad?"

"Not good. But I came in here, Lieutenant, sir, to say that luncheon is now being served. Chow down, in other words."

Ken folded the chart and papers and put them back into the envelope before climbing down. As Malone stood aside to let him out, he asked, "Where's the mess hall?"

"The mess hall? If you mean where do we eat, we eat where we play acey-deucy, shoot the breeze, navigate, operate, caulk off, study, read, listen to the radio, and where one of my many bosses, the communicator, sleeps. The wardroom."

As they walked down the narrow corridor, Ken said, "My name is Ken. What's yours?"

Malone laughed. "It's Patrick Ignatius MacGonigle Malone, Jr. But most people call me Pat if they're friendly."

"OK, Pat. Now what's your job on the boat?"

"Me? Well, being junior officer aboard, I get all the

46

dirty details no one else wants. Officially I'm the Assistant Communications and Sound Officer. I'm also Assistant to the Assistant Approach Officer, the Assistant Engineering Officer, the Assistant Diving Officer, the Assistant Gunnery and Torpedo Officer. I am also Mess Treasurer without assistant, and acey-deucy player without peer."

When they got to the wardroom two other officers were already there. Malone introduced Ken to Lieutenant (j.g.) Silas Mount and to Lieutenant Philip Carney. "Si is the First Lieutenant of the Boat as well as Gunnery and Torpedo Officer," Malone told him, "And Phil Carney is the Exec and Assistant Approach Officer."

"And Navigator," Carney said, "unless, of course, Pat, you'd like to navigate this trip?"

Ken squeezed around the table and sat down between Silas Mount and Malone. "I'm afraid I've cluttered up your cabin, Mr. Mount," Ken told him. "I've got a lot of diving gear stowed in there."

"Forget it, Ken," Mount said pleasantly. "Nothing can be worse than the mere fact of having to live in the same boat with Malone."

"Hear, hear," Malone said.

"By the way," Mount went on, "which bunk did Malone give you?"

"The top one," Ken told him.

Mount raised his voice so the officers coming in could hear. "Outrageous! Did you hear that, gentlemen? *Ensign* Malone has had the audacity to assign a lieutenant (j.g.) to the top bunk. Absolutely unwarranted assumption of authority."

Malone spoke quietly to Ken. "Pay no attention to him, Ken. As you know, being an ensign is merely a constant battle for mere survival, that's all."

Ken, who had come into the Navy as a j.g., said nothing.

As the food was brought in by a steward, the officers

47

spent their spare time, when not eating, in ribbing Malone.

Ken, after the reception Stevenson had given him, began to feel better. With these officers there was a spirit of comradeship and of genuine friendship. Through all the ribbing you could tell that they all liked Malone—and liked each other. Ken wondered how Stevenson fitted in with them?

For a moment he studied Silas Mount, his other roommate. Mount was a thin-faced man of about twenty-four. His hair was jet black, his eyes a dark blue, and his whole expression was sensitive, intelligent. With a flowing black tie he could pose as a poet.

Philip Carney, on the other hand, had a strong, alert, quiet face. Ken noticed that, at every different sound in the submarine, Carney would stop eating or talking and listen. He seemed to be always conscious of what was happening in the boat.

Stevenson didn't come down off the bridge until the others had almost finished lunch. As he came in they stood up as well as they could and waited until he sat down.

Carney, the Executive Officer, asked, "How's it going, Skipper?"

Stevenson ignored him and said, to Ken, "Where is the op plan, Mr. Braden?"

"In my cabin, sir."

Stevenson stopped helping himself, the spoon halfway to his plate. For a moment he stared across the small table at Ken and then said coldly, "Go and get it."

Ken had a hard time getting over the other officers' legs. In the cabin he stood for a moment looking down at the floor. His hands had started shaking and his stomach felt gone.

Back in the wardroom with the SCAN envelope he listened as Stevenson said, "From now on, Mr. Braden,

48

the op plan stays in your *hands* or locked in my desk. *Nowhere* else."

"I'm sorry, sir," Ken said, meaning it and knowing that he had been careless.

When Ken was back in his seat, Stevenson looked at the officers around the table. "All right, gentlemen, here's the picture. After a refueling stop at Midway, we are going out to the mid-Pacific. I can't tell you exactly what we're looking for but, since that is no concern of the boat itself, it doesn't matter. We've got some islands to go to and Mr. Braden, our passenger, will do a little exploring. It seems that Mr. Braden is some sort of underwater expert.

"As far as the boat is concerned, there's only one important thing. We must get to the islands and get back. Is that clear, gentlemen?"

Only the Exec spoke. "Does that mean that if a really good target—a carrier or a battlewagon, say—shows up we've got to leave it alone, Skipper?"

"Exactly," Stevenson said. "This is not a war patrol. This is a recon patrol. There will be no—repeat, no—hunting for targets."

The Exec spoke again. "Suppose we're attacked, sir?"

"We hit the coral and stay there," Stevenson told him.

"What about after the recon, Skipper? Can we hunt then?"

"We return to Pearl and make our report."

The officers were silent for a moment. Disappointment was heavy on them as they finished eating and, one by one, drifted out of the room.

CHAPTER 2

KEN WAS STILL STUDYING THE OP PLAN when, at a little after four in the afternoon, Malone came into the cabin.

"How's it going, Pat?"

"When I am on watch all goes well, sir. Things only get fouled up when those beastly lieutenants take over the boat. We'll probably sink before eight bells rings again."

Ken sat up in his bunk. "I need some help, Pat. What do you have to do for the next hour or so?"

"Nothing. We stand watches four on and eight off. What can I do for you?"

"Well, here's the picture. I've got to get ashore on those islands."

"We've got a rubber boat," Malone told him.

"I'd better not use that. Too easy to see. I'll have to go under water right up to the beach and then see what cooks."

Malone glanced at him. "Swimming?"

Ken nodded.

"Alone?"

Ken nodded again.

"What about sharks? Barracuda?"

"Sharks never bothered anybody at the training school and we saw a lot of 'em. Apparently they react differently to men when they're down under the water with them. I don't know about barracuda. But most fish don't seem to pay much attention to you when you're down there with 'em. It's only when you break the surface that they react very much."

"Oh well, I guess when you see a shark or something you can get out of his way, can't you?"

"I won't be able to see them," Ken told him.

"Can't you see out of that face mask?" Malone asked, surprised.

"Sure. In the daytime."

Malone looked up at him again. "You mean you're going in that water at *night?*"

"I think so, Pat. I'd be too easy to spot coming in in daylight. And once I'm caught, or even seen, the whole thing blows up."

Malone shook his head slowly. "Man, I wouldn't get in that water at night for anybody in the Navy. I've seen some horrible-looking things in this ocean."

"I don't suppose I look particularly pretty to them, either, with all that gear on. But that's not the first problem. What worries me is how close to a beach can this boat go? I mean, submerged?"

"Depends on the Skipper," Malone told him. "Mush Morton took the *Wahoo* right into Wewak Harbor."

"Distance gets important if there's lots of it. I can lug a maximum of four hours' worth of oxygen or air but I can't lug it far. Even if I could there's the problem of time. If the boat can't get in close to the beach I won't have time to swim ashore, look around, and swim back in one night."

"What do you call 'close'?"

"I call a mile a long way."

"A mile from an enemy coast isn't a long way to a submarine," Malone said. "But the whole thing depends on how deep the water is. If we've got to go in submerged then we'll need at the very least sixty feet of water between top and bottom. I don't think the Skipper'll want to go into water less than a hundred feet deep unless he *absolutely* has to."

Ken climbed down from his bunk with the SCAN chart. "Here're the islands, Pat."

Malone studied the chart and began to shake his head. "The depths aren't very well marked. See, there's nothing to show how deep the water is in the lagoon here."

"They told me at school that the water inside the lagoon of an atoll is usually deeper than the water close in around the outside of it."

"I guess that's true. The islands are always being built up by coral on the outside and rotting away on the inside," Malone agreed, still studying the chart. "But, boy, that's a narrow little slit we'll have to get through to get inside. If we got into any trouble in there all the Japoons would have to do would be to put a boat right here"—he pointed to the open water between two of the islands—"and let us have it when we tried to get out again. Like shooting fish in a barrel."

Looking across the chart at the bearded ensign, Ken asked, "Do you think Stevenson would go in through there?"

Malone glanced at the open doorway and said in a whisper, "Always call him 'Skipper,' Ken, or 'Captain.'"

Ken nodded. "Thanks. Well, would he?"

"It's not impossible, Ken," Malone said slowly, "but, man, oh, man, it would take a real cool character to do it."

"I don't see any other way," Ken said at last. "We'll have to go inside the lagoon."

"*If* the Skipper'll do it," Malone reminded him.

"If he won't I don't see how I can get ashore. Surf is hard to handle even on a sandy beach. Breaking over a coral reef is sort of rough on you."

"How much do those tanks and all that gear weigh?"

"Nothing—when you're under the water. But plenty when you're trying to walk out of surf."

Malone got up and inspected his beard in the mirror. "I'm beginning to think that I've made a little mistake, Ken, boy. From what the Skipper said in the wardroom I figured this was going to be a joy ride. A no-dive trip out and back, with nothing coming down around our ears. Now I've got this little old feeling that I'm wrong."

"Maybe the Japs haven't got a thing on this atoll. Maybe we'll slip in and slip out without any trouble at all."

"Maybe," Malone said. "But I've got this little old feeling. Right here . . ." He let his knees wobble together.

Ken laughed and then said seriously, "Problem number two: how do I get in and get out of this boat?"

"Submerged or on the surface?"

"Submerged."

"That's fairly simple. Go out the escape hatch."

"How would I get back in again?"

"Same way."

"Now," Ken said, "problem three——"

"For a lieutenant, boy, you sure got problems," Malone said. "What's this one?"

"How do I find this boat under the water?"

Malone pulled at his beard. "How well can you see under water?"

"At night? Not at all. And all of this has got to be done at night."

Malone sighed. He got the chart down off Ken's bunk and studied it. "There wouldn't be much current inside the lagoon," he decided. "So maybe we wouldn't drift far from where you left us."

"Can't you just let a sub go down to the bottom and rest there?"

"The answer is yes. But there aren't any skippers who'll do it on purpose. Especially on coral. You can do a lot of damage to the valves and even the props. Also, it's deep in that lagoon—maybe three or four hundred feet. How would you get down there—if we could?"

"I can go down three hundred—if I *have* to," Ken told him.

53

Malone put the chart back and plucked at his beard. "How well can you hear under water?"

"When I stop breathing I can hear as well as or better than I can in the open air."

"I think that's the only answer. We could hang the boat just under the water and try to keep her in one spot. Then, if the sound of the motors and things isn't enough, we could signal in some way—maybe whang on the hull with a hammer?"

"I should be able to hear that. We ought to give this whole plan a dry run pretty soon and work the bugs out of it."

Malone started to say something when a messenger told him the Exec wanted to see him.

"Some weighty problem that needs an ensign," Malone said, going out.

Alone again, Ken went on studying the op plan. There was among the papers a thin booklet which described the islands. The greatest height above sea level was on Midnight Island and was only twelve feet. As the chart showed, there was a fringing reef on the seaward side of all the islands and this reef extended out for almost a mile. The vegetation consisted mostly of coconut trees, pandanus, breadfruit, and a low scrub. The soil was sandy, the climate tropical, with the temperature usually in the eighties.

The islands had been, until they were overrun by the Japanese in 1941, under British administration. The people were Micronesian, with slanted, Malay-type eyes, dark brown skin. They were smaller than Polynesians. Although they had a language of their own they usually spoke English, and it was assumed that they were still friendly to America and Britain, although there was no information about how the Japanese had treated them since taking over. They lived on fish, a root called tannia, coconuts, an occasional pig, and breadfruit. They were fair seamen but could not compare with the Polynesians.

They were, Ken read, a peaceful, lazy people without much ambition, who lived in open, thatched houses with thin leaf walls.

The population prior to 1941 on this atoll was 298 people.

Ken put all the papers back in the SCAN package and stretched out on his bunk. Trying to plan his movements when they reached the atoll brought him up against a blank wall. There was nothing he could work out until he knew whether Stevenson would go into the lagoon.

As he was lying there a gong rang somewhere in the boat. Ken jerked upright.

Then the lights went out.

He scrambled down out of the bunk in the darkness, but before he got to the floor, the lights came on again.

Only now instead of being bright and white they were a ghostly red.

Ken, scared, stepped out into the corridor and stopped a passing sailor. "What's the trouble? What's going on?"

"Why, nothing, Lieutenant," the sailor said.

"Why the gong? Why all this red light?"

"Night adaptation, Lieutenant," the sailor said, going on down the corridor.

CHAPTER 3

KEN WAS STILL STANDING IN THE CORRIDOR when his other roommate, Silas Mount, came along. Ken followed him back into the cabin.

"I guess I'm stupid, but what's the red light for?"

"Night adaptation, Ken," Mount told him, getting ready to brush his teeth. "It's dark now."

"What's dark?"

Silas looked over his shoulder at him. "The night, Ken. The sky."

"Oh," Ken said, feeling foolish. Then he laughed. "You know, I haven't been on deck since I came aboard. I'd forgotten all about day and night."

"Neither have I. And about the only way you can tell is when we rig for red. Then it's night outside. We do that so that if we have to go topside to man the guns or stand watch our eyes will already be adjusted to the darkness by this red light. We'll be able to see right away."

Ken sat down on Si's bunk. "What do you do aboard ship?" he asked as Mount finished cleaning his teeth.

"Oh, I'm the fish, firecracker, and dirty-detail officer. I try to make these torpedoes of ours run straight and go off when they're supposed to, and I look after the deck and machine guns. Officially, I guess I'm the Gunnery and Torpedo Officer and the First Lieutenant."

"Sounds like quite a job."

"It isn't bad. Pat Malone's the one with the tough one. He's assistant something to just about everybody and Mess Treasurer, too, so he gets *all* the gripes."

The steward stuck his head into the cabin. "Lieutenant Braden, the Skipper says he wants you *right now.*"

Ken grabbed the SCAN envelope. Now, he thought, I can get the answer to that question. Now I can really start planning this thing. It made him feel good—as though a weight had been lifted from his shoulders.

He knocked, and Stevenson told him to come in. Ken drew the curtain as Stevenson swiveled around in the chair and held out his hand. Ken gave him the SCAN envelope.

"Where's your op plan, Mr. Braden?"

"Sir, I can't make any plans until I find out whether or not you'll take the boat into the lagoon at the atoll."

"It seems to me that I told you to have a written op plan ready by twenty hundred, Mr. Braden. It is now twenty hundred."

Ken felt helpless; felt as though he were tangled up in some sort of invisible web. "Sir, I can't make a plan without knowing what you will do. Don't you think, sir, that if we work on this thing together we'll do a lot better?"

"Mr. Braden, my job is to run my submarine. Your job is to find that code. Those are separate and distinct operations. I will take you where you want to go. After that, it's up to you. Is that clear?"

"Yes, sir."

"Check! Now it seems to me that even a reserve officer should be able to make a plan of what he's going to do and submit it to his commanding officer."

"Yes, sir. Then I can assume that you *will* go into the lagoon?"

"What lagoon?"

Ken got out the chart and showed him the lagoon with the islands ringing it.

Stevenson sat for a long time looking at the chart. Finally he said, "I see no reason to put my boat into that trap, Mr. Braden. Do you realize that the Japs could have that entrance rigged with a net, or have it mined? That they could let us in and then slam the door on us?" He looked up at Ken. "Did you actually think—even for a moment—that I would take my boat into a place like that?"

"I hoped so, sir. With the boat in the lagoon I can get ashore very easily and——"

"Very easily," Stevenson interrupted him. "Is your ease and comfort the main thing here, Mr. Braden?"

"No, sir," Ken said, trying not to let any anger sound in his voice. "But if I try to get ashore from the seaward side it would mean a long swim. Then, too, a coral reef like this one is dangerous if there's any surf breaking on it at all."

"Didn't you realize that there would be danger, Mr. Braden?"

"Of course, sir. But since there's a good deal of unavoidable danger after I get ashore, why add unnecessary danger *trying* to get there?"

"It seems to me that you're confining your thoughts to the danger to yourself, Mr. Braden, and not giving very much thought to the men and officers in this boat. It seems to me that you're perfectly willing to risk all their lives so that you won't have the inconvenience of crossing a little shelf of coral."

Ken almost gave up as he looked at Stevenson's washed-out blue eyes, in which he could find no sympathy, no understanding of the problem. "Perhaps so, sir. I'm sorry. Then we'll plan on approaching the islands from the seaward side? Will you give me some idea how close to the reef you will bring the boat, sir?"

Stevenson studied the chart, then, with dividers, took some measurements. Ken felt sick as he saw the points of the dividers opening wider and wider. At last Stevenson said, "Five thousand yards, Mr. Braden."

Ken's whole body went slack. Three miles. Three *miles*. In the open ocean.

During UDT he had had to swim a mile with fins but no diving gear. He had made it in forty-five minutes and still remembered how bushed he had been at the end of it. Now—three miles in probably rough water, at night, with tanks and fifteen pounds of lead in the belt. . . .

"That would take approximately three hours, sir. Just to reach the reef. I don't know how long it would take me to cross it and get the gear hidden. Say half an hour. That would mean going and coming would take around seven hours. That wouldn't leave me much time during darkness to explore the island, sir."

Stevenson looked up at him. "I am not concerned with that, Mr. Braden. As I said before, my job is to run my boat, yours is to get to the islands. If it takes you seven hours or twenty hours is not my concern. Do you understand?"

"Don't you think you could come in a little closer, sir?"

"Do you see this line of shading, Mr. Braden?" he asked, pointing on the chart with the dividers. "The water there is sixty feet deep. I will not take my boat into water less than sixty feet. Is that clear?"

"Yes, sir."

"Right! Check! Now, if I'm not mistaken, the distance from that line to the reef is"—he measured again with the dividers on the side of the chart—"five thousand yards, give a yard or two one way or the other. Right?"

"Yes, sir."

"So there's your answer, Mr. Braden. Five thousand yards. Now take this op plan and, this time, *write* a detailed plan of your own. Have it ready by oh eight hundred in the morning."

"Aye, aye, sir."

Ken had been back in his cabin only a few minutes when Malone came in, his beard odd-looking in the dim red light. He was carrying two enormous sandwiches. "Want?" he asked.

"No, thanks," Ken said.

Malone stopped in the middle of a bite and looked up at him. Swallowing, he said, "You look sort of sunk, boy. What's the trouble? Don't tell me you're seasick."

"No. But I'm sunk all right. The Skipper says he won't go inside the lagoon. The nearest he'll come is five thousand yards on the outside."

Malone whistled softly. "Isn't that kind of a long pull for you?"

Ken nodded.

"Was the Skipper really firm about this?"

"Like a rock."

Malone gnawed on his sandwiches, taking bites out of each one. "The only man aboard who can talk with the Skipper is Phil Carney."

"The Exec?"

Malone nodded, finishing his sandwiches and combing the crumbs out of his beard. "Let's go talk to Phil."

"All right." Ken climbed down out of his bunk as Malone, still brushing his beard, said, "Phil's the best submariner in the boat. If he thinks the boat can be taken into the lagoon he might be able to change the Skipper's mind about it."

Carney was in his cabin dressing.

Ken showed him the chart and explained the problem.

Carney was a rugged, blond man with short, bristly, sandy hair. There were crow's feet lines at the corner of his blue eyes and a livid scar running from his forehead down to his throat. You could feel determination in him, and a great calmness. He'd be hard to panic, Ken thought, watching him read the chart. And tough to fight.

At last he began to shake his head. Ken's hopes died.

"I wouldn't take a boat in there unless I had to," he said quietly. "But then I don't see all the picture, Ken. What's wrong with standing off five thousand?"

Ken felt at once that talking with Carney was entirely different from talking with Stevenson. Carney's mind was open; Stevenson's was closed. Carney listened and thought about the problem as a whole while Stevenson thought only about where he fitted into it.

"Well, sir," Ken said, "first, there's the time element. According to the dope, there'll only be about six hours of real darkness out there at this time of year. If I have to swim ten thousand yards there won't be any darkness left to work in.

"Next, there's the problem of getting across the surf. I realize that I sound like a baby crying about that, but if I don't make it, this whole mission gets to be useless.

"Next, there's a smaller problem of finding the boat when I come back. Every yard increases the chance for error. You know a man in the water can't see very far so I only have to miss the boat by a few yards and I've had it. Which also makes the mission useless."

Carney put on his cap. "I'm going up on the bridge. Let's hash it out up there."

Ken and Pat followed him as he went aft and then up through the control room to the conning tower. There, in the dim red light, the helmsman was at the big bronze wheel, the talkers and other watchstanders were silent in the darkness. The radar watch was hunched over the faint green dial with the thin bright line sweeping slowly around and around.

Carney said nothing as he went on up the ladder, but Ken had seen the way he had glanced at everything in the conning tower before going on.

They followed him out of the small hatch and the blast of damp, cool night air hit them in the face.

It was a beautiful, calm, starry night. Six or seven men were on the bridge, with two more in the lookout cages up on the periscope structure. No one was talking.

Carney went over to the Officer of the Deck and asked how things were going.

"Very well. That battery leak is fixed and so is the hoist, Phil."

"Any word from the Skipper?"

"Only the night order book. Nothing else."

Carney said quietly, "I'd be on my toes for a drill before morning, Frank. We've been steaming a long time with no drills."

"Thanks. What do you think about some dives tomorrow, too?"

"I'll talk to the Skipper about it. We were getting under the water too slowly back there a while ago."

"I know it. The last dive took thirty seconds from horn to green board."

Ken, standing behind them, didn't even know what they were talking about. He had thought that after the months of indoctrination he could at least recognize the Navy's way of talking but he had certainly never heard of a green board and wondered now what it meant.

Carney turned away and led them back to a small wooden seat aft. "You can smoke back here if you want to, but the smoking lamp's out up here after we leave Midway," he said, lighting a cigarette.

Ken sat on one side of him, Malone on the other. Ken still had the SCAN package but there wasn't enough starlight to see the chart.

"The Skipper's right about that five thousand," Carney said. "You'd be asking for it to come in any closer. Coral is rough on submarines. So that leaves nothing but the lagoon."

"Mush took *Wahoo* into Wewak," Malone said. "That entrance was a lot shallower than this one and Wewak's a big base. We didn't see any signs of nets or booms or mines."

Carney said quietly, "Mush isn't running this boat."

"And I heard that Donc Donaho took a boat into the lagoon at Truk," Malone went on. "Truk's the biggest base they've got out here, so if that isn't mined or netted I don't think they'd go to all the trouble of mining or netting the entrance to that little old lagoon where they haven't got a thing but some sand and naked natives."

"I don't think so, either," Carney agreed. "But here's an item. The water in those lagoons is usually calm and clear as a bell. A plane flying over it could see us even if we were a hundred, maybe two hundred, feet down. So there we are, fat, dumb, and happy, not even knowing a plane is up there looking at us."

"We wouldn't have to stay there during daylight," Ken reminded him.

"No, I guess not." Carney flipped his cigarette in a long arc down to the black, rushing water. "Five thousand yards," he said slowly, talking to himself. "That's a long haul." He suddenly stood up. "Well, if I can catch the Skipper in a good humor I'll talk to him about it."

"What'll you say, Phil?" Malone asked.

Carney stood for a moment looking at the black water turning white as the propellers churned into it. Then he sighed. "Well, based on the information we've got on the chart, I'd take a chance. That is, if I was commanding this piece of stovepipe—which I ain't. On the other hand, these charts have turned out to be all wrong a lot of times. Until this war started the Pacific Ocean was, in a lot of places, unknown; never charted. You don't know until you get there. Remember *Trigger* going on the reef during the battle at Midway, Pat?"

Ken, hope coming up in him—a little—wanted to get it straight. "Do you mean, sir, that if you were Skipper you'd take the boat into the lagoon?"

Carney scrubbed his bristly hair with one hand. "If it's like it is on the chart, the boat could get in, Ken."

"Will you try to talk the Skipper into seeing it that way, sir?"

Carney went on scrubbing his head. Finally he said, "Yes."

Malone and Ken watched him go forward and disappear down the hatch.

Malone said quietly, "He'll make a good skipper someday, if they ever give him a boat. I'd go in any boat with him."

"He seems a lot older than most lieutenants," Ken said.

"He is. He's thirty. You know, he enlisted in the Navy right after Pearl Harbor. Just walked into a recruiting office and signed up.

"Then, right after boot camp, he signed up for the boats. You know, all hands in the boats have to volunteer for them. There aren't any people in the boats who don't *want* to be in 'em. So Phil asked for subs and then, in New London, somebody got smart and made him an officer. An *ensign*, if you please. So he's come all the way. He's had twenty, thirty patrols and been everything in the boats except Skipper. He almost got it in *Tang*; laid his face open and just missed his jugular.

"I think he's right in there with Mush and the rest of the top Joes. Of course, that's just guessing because you can't ever tell what a man's going to be like once he makes Skipper. I've seen good execs turn into lousy skippers. But I don't think Phil would. He's too steady. Commanding a boat wouldn't shake him at all."

"That must be the loneliest job in the world," Ken decided. "Well, I hope Phil can talk our Skipper into going into that lagoon. Otherwise I'm a dead pigeon." He stood up. "So now I've got the rest of the night to write a detailed plan—based on five thousand yards. By the way, where can I find a space big enough to lay down a sheet of paper?"

"The wardroom's the only place. Just tell the acey-deucy players to give you some room."

Ken took a last long breath of the fresh, cool, salty air and went back down the hatch into the red glow of the submarine.

CHAPTER 4

As THE NIGHT WORE ON THE OTHER OFFICERS finished reading or writing or working around the wardroom table
and drifted off, either to go on watch or to sleep. At last
Ken was alone there with his problem.

He kept on writing down his plan although he knew
that it was useless.

First, he wrote, there should be a general reconnais-
sance of the atoll. The submarine could move at periscope depth in as close as possible and study each of the
islands. If, by doing that, any sign of a radio station
was found it would save a lot of useless searching.

Second, if nothing was sighted through the periscope,
Ken would have to start searching each island.

As he wrote he felt as though he were trying to stuff
smoke into a bottle. He carefully detailed each of his
movements and the maneuvers of the sub, but long
before his time schedule got him back to the boat the
night would be gone.

There simply was not enough *time*. The nights were
not long enough.

Around two in the morning the steward stuck his head
through the little opening from the galley. "You want
some jamoke, Mr. Braden?" he asked.

"Some what?"

"Jamoke. Joe. Java. Boiler compound. Coffee?"

"Please."

"I'll fix 'em. How you like? We got sugar, cream, milk,
anything."

"Just plain, please. What's your name?"

66

"Willy Armstrong."

"How long have you been in submarines?"

"One thousand years, sir. Here you go." Willy shoved a cup of coffee through the opening. "I'll make you a sandwich, too."

"No, thanks. This is fine. How'd you get in submarines, Willy?"

"Me? Well, sir, I went downtown one Saturday and this fellow says, 'Boy, you better join the Navy before the Army catches you.' And I told him I didn't know the Army was even *after* me but he says they were and that if I'd rather ride than walk I'd better join the Navy. So I did.

"Next thing you know I'm on this airplane carrier. And next thing you know here come a bunch of Jap airplanes and they drop some bombs on us and shoot us up pretty bad. Fact is, we sink.

"So when they pulled me out of the water I said to myself, I'm going where those airplanes can't see me. So I got in submarines. Nobody can see you but, man, they can sure hear you down there. *Click bam swish swish swish*. Man, that's a noise I don't *ever* want to hear again. I don't even want to hear that *peem peem peem*."

Ken was about to ask what all this was about when a gong began to ring with a frantic, hurrying sound.

"Oh-oh," Willy said. "I've been expecting this."

"What is it?"

Before Willy could answer a voice from the loud-speaker said, "Battle stations submerged."

Then there were a lot of noises and commands.

Through all this then came the sound of a harsh, old-fashioned automobile horn. It went *ah-ooh-gah, ah-ooh-gah*.

Then Stevenson's voice saying, "Dive the boat."

"Are we going under?" Ken asked Willy.

"We're going to try," Willy said as he ran into the

wardroom and put his hand on a valve on the wall. "We're sure going to try."

"Flood negative. Flood safety."

"Hatch secured, sir."

"Close induction."

"Green board. Green board."

"Bleed air."

Ken felt the deck tilt a little forward and then he felt a slight pressure of air against his eardrums.

Someone said, "Air in the boat, sir."

"Eight degrees down bubble."

"Easy on the bow planes. *Easy!*"

"Blow negative."

"All ahead one third."

Gradually the noise and the orders stopped. Now, though, instead of the heavy pulsing of the diesels that Ken had gotten used to hearing and feeling there was a new, high, whining sound.

"When are we going to go down, Willy?" Ken asked.

"We're down, sir. At least, we're supposed to be down." He looked at the dial on the wall. "We're down to sixty feet. But we're going to hear from the Skipper about it."

"Why?" Ken asked.

Before Willy could answer, Stevenson's voice came over the loud-speaker. It had a distant, disgusted sound. "That dive was as lousy as any I've ever seen in the boats," he said, his voice going into every part of the ship. "I didn't get a green board for thirty-seven seconds. It took sixteen seconds to clear the bridge and close the hatch. I want that down to eleven seconds. Just simply lousy, gentlemen."

Willy whispered, "I *told* you we were going to hear from him."

Stevenson's voice started again. "Now bring her up and do it again. I want this boat down sixty feet in fifty seconds."

Again the horn blew, orders sounded throughout the boat, and soon Ken could hear water pouring down the hull as the *Shark* broke the surface.

Willy went back into the little galley and Ken could see him making sandwiches and coffee. "We're going to be doing this all night long," he declared. "And all day too."

As the rest of the crew practiced diving, Ken went on, hopelessly, writing his op plan.

At four in the morning he finished the thing and leaned back. Slowly, like something stepping out of a fog bank, he began to realize that what he had written on those pieces of paper was—simply—his death warrant. Up until now he had thought of this op plan of his as only a ridiculous set of plans written merely to satisfy the whim of a petulant, disagreeable man. But now, like a blow—like a fist in the mouth—he knew that this same man would use these nonsensical plans; would put him in the open ocean, in the dark, three miles from a hostile island. His chances of getting back to the *Shark* were—exactly—zero.

Through the mist of his fatigue and fear Ken gradually saw Stevenson not as a lieutenant commander in the Navy, not even as a man. Stevenson became, in Ken's mind, his executioner, his murderer.

And there was, now, nothing Ken could do about it.

He was so absorbed in his own despair that he didn't notice Carney come in; didn't even hear him ask Willy for a cup of coffee.

Willy's cheerful voice brought Ken's mind back into the wardroom. "Coming right up, Mr. Carney. How we doing?"

"Better, but still lousy. Seventy on the last one."

"That's real lousy," Willy agreed, bringing in the coffee.

As Carney sipped it he looked across at Ken. "No soap," he said quietly.

Ken looked up.

"I talked to the Skipper. He won't take the boat into the lagoon, Ken."

Ken shrugged. "Well, thanks, anyway."

"He's got a point," Carney said. "It's a dangerous slot to go into."

Ken nodded.

"How're you coming with your op plan?"

Ken looked steadily across the green table at him. "It's finished, but it won't work. Are we going to dive some more?"

"We're through for the night. But it sure is lousy. Good thing nobody's trying to ash-can us—we'd never get under in time. Why won't it work, Ken?"

"The nights aren't long enough."

Willy came in with some sandwiches. "We through for tonight, sir?"

"All through."

"That's good. We're just a little weary, that's all. A little weary. Tomorrow we'll get to clicking better."

"I hope so," Carney said. "What's in these sandwiches —shoe leather?"

"No, sir. Couldn't get any shoe leather this trip."

Carney got up with a sandwich in his hand. "What can you do about it, Ken?"

"Nothing." Ken gathered up his papers and rose. "Good night, sir. Night, Willy."

Carney stood looking at the door through which Ken had gone. Willy came in and said, "Mr. Braden looks like he's been talking to a ghost."

"Poor guy," Carney said.

"He looks like a nine-of-spades man to me," Willy said.

"What's that, Willy?"

"Old Man Death mighty close to nine-of-spades people. Mighty close. But I tell you who the *real* nine-of-spades man is—the Skipper."

"I don't believe in that stuff, Willy."

"I don't either. Just something to talk about."

Carney looked at him. "It isn't even much to talk about, Willy. Nor think about, either."

"No, sir. I guess you're right."

As Ken went into his cabin he saw that Si Mount was already asleep in the lowest bunk. But Pat Malone was down on his knees on the deck.

Ken waited in the doorway until Malone finished praying.

"Sorry to keep you waiting," Pat said, standing up.

"You didn't," Ken told him. Then, as he started to undress, he said slowly, "I wish I could pray some."

"Go ahead, Ken."

"No. I should have done it a long time ago. If I do it now maybe God would think I was only praying because I'm in a jam."

Pat got into his bunk. "Well, I do my praying now while it's quiet because when the depth charges start coming down around your ears you don't have time. But then I figure that the Lord knows what He's doing, so that if you started to pray now He could make up His mind what to do about it."

Ken reached for the light switch. "All set?"

"Douse 'em," Malone told him.

Ken turned out the lights. Then, in the darkness of the cabin, he got down on his knees on the cold steel deck and prayed.

Ken turned in his op plan at eight o'clock. Stevenson took it without a word and dismissed him.

Ken spent the rest of the morning studying the Japanese ideographs; writing down the little crooked symbols and trying to remember which ones stood for what.

When Stevenson came in for lunch he smiled at Ken. Then he reached out and patted him on the shoulder.

"That's better, Mr. Braden," he said pleasantly. "That's a pretty good op plan. There are a few changes I want made—I've made notes in the margin. But it isn't too bad, as a start."

"Thank you, sir," Ken said, wondering how Stevenson could think like that. Sure, there were a lot of plans, a lot of details of time and movement, but the whole thing was as meaningless as the jabbering of an idiot.

Then, suddenly, Ken began to wonder. As Stevenson took his napkin out of the ring, Ken watched him. Perhaps, he thought, there was a way out of this mess.

At the end of the meal Stevenson announced to the officers at the table that they were going to practice diving for the rest of the afternoon. "In fact," he went on, "we're going to dive this boat from now until we reach sixty feet in fifty seconds. Is that clear?"

The officers nodded.

"Right! Check!" Stevenson said, leaving the room.

Phil Carney was sitting next to Ken. For a long time after the Skipper left he just sat, his hands around his coffee mug. Finally he raised his head. "What's the matter with us?"

Si Mount said, "Phil, there's just no spirit in the boat. The men are trying. When you're in your division it looks like every man is doing his job all right. But there's just a little time lag here and there."

Frank Doherty, the Engineering Officer, said, "We act like we're playing around off New London, Connecticut, U.S.A. In a couple of days we'll be west of Midway and right under the gun. We're going to get our heads knocked off if we don't start handling this boat right."

Carney slowly nodded his head and gripped his coffee mug. "Gents," he said, "let's get behind the Skipper and get this boat under the water *right*. Let's forget our personal feelings and go to work. I hate to be corny, but the life you save isn't going to be anybody else's—it's going to be yours. Maybe."

No one said anything. One by one they filed out, leaving Ken alone in the wardroom.

All afternoon the boat submerged, stayed below awhile, and then came back to the surface, only to submerge again.

Ken stayed in the wardroom studying the Japanese numbers until, at last, he heard Stevenson saying over the PA system, "That's a little less lousy, men. Secure from general quarters."

Soon Pat came into the wardroom. He looked a lot more cheerful now. "That's better. We're smoothing out a little. How's it going, boy?" he asked, tapping Ken on the shoulder.

"*Hitotsu, futatsu, mitsu, yotsu . . .*"

"Come againsu?"

CHAPTER 5

FROM THEN UNTIL THEY REACHED Midway Island, Ken either studied Japanese, corrected his op plan, or worked with the Minox cameras.

The Minox wasn't much bigger than a pack of chewing gum but, Ken found, it was an extraordinary machine. No wonder, he thought, they called it the "spy camera."

With Willy's help he set up a small darkroom in the service pantry where he could develop the pictures he took. Then, in as many different degrees of light as he could find, he took photographs of all sorts of papers and writing. The Minox pictures were tiny but, with a magnifying glass, he could see that they were extraordinarily sharp and clear even when the writing on the paper was thin and the light poor. With the extremely fast film he had he was now sure that he could get a picture of the code—if he found it—with only the dimmest light.

Satisfied with the Minox and with the watertight case for it, Ken checked over his other gear. Somehow oil had gotten on some of the fittings of the rebreather outfit. This scared him for a moment for he had seen what happens when pure oxygen under two thousand pounds pressure comes in contact with oil. The explosion is instantaneous and violent, blasting the lungs out of whoever is wearing the rebreather when it happens.

The Chief of the Boat took over there, though, and cleaned off every trace of oil. But, just to be sure, Ken took the outfit up to the flying bridge one afternoon and tested it, letting oxygen slowly into the bag until he was certain that there wasn't going to be any explosion when he went under water with the thing.

The night before they got to Midway, Ken found Si and Pat Malone both in their bunks, but neither one asleep. As he came into the tiny cabin he had a feeling that they had been talking about something and had abruptly stopped when he came in. This made him feel uncomfortable—as though they had been telling secrets and didn't want him to know.

He undressed without saying anything and climbed on up to his high bunk. Si asked, "All set?" and Pat said, "All set, Ken?"

"Douse 'em."

For a long time after the lights went out there was no sound from Si or Pat, but when Ken thought they must be asleep, Pat suddenly asked, "Ken, you awake?"

"Yeah."

"I've been wondering if the Skipper has changed his mind about going inside the lagoon."

"No, he hasn't."

There was then another long pause before Pat said quietly, "We're in trouble, Ken."

"What sort of trouble?"

"All sorts. Si and I were talking about it when you came in, and at first, we thought that there was no use crying on your shoulder about it. But since you're up to your neck in it anyhow, you might as well get the whole picture."

"All right," Ken said, "what is it?"

"The Skipper," Malone said. "The men aren't with him. That's BIG trouble in a submarine. In the surface Navy it's sort of different. Each man is freer up there, each man can do more or less what he wants to. Say a carrier is getting dive-bombed. Well, the scared guys, the cowards, can jump off. But there's no jumping off in a sub. When we start getting a working over we're all in here together and we've got to stay in here until it's either over and the boat is still in one piece or—the sea comes in.

"We're stuck. Stuck with a scared Skipper and a scared crew. You know something, Si? I don't think we're ever going to get back to Pearl Harbor. It's a feeling in my bones or somewhere. I think we're going to catch it this trip. Catch *all* of it."

"No use thinking like that, Pat," Si told him. "That'll just give you the blues. In fact, a scared skipper and a scared crew stand a better chance of getting back because he won't take us into any trouble. Ken up there is the only one who's liable to catch it."

"Oh well," Ken said, "as they say in the Marine Corps, 'Who wants to live forever?'"

"Me," Malone said. "In fact, forever isn't long enough. If there's one thing I really love, it's living."

"I don't object to sleeping, either," Si said. "And I'm going to do some of it right now."

Soon both Pat and Si were asleep. Ken, feeling more alone in that cramped room than he had ever felt in his life, couldn't sleep.

What, he wondered, was the difference between a brave man and a coward?

And, he wondered, was Stevenson really scared? Was he, really, a coward? Or was he just a man with a little mind? A man who couldn't see his way through all the rigmarole of the Navy? Who couldn't see the forest for the trees? Or was Stevenson so busy with his own career and advancement in the Navy, so careful not to hurt it, that he would take no chances at all?

There were no answers to any of those questions.

So Ken began to wonder if *he* was a brave man or a coward.

There was no answer to that, either.

They took on fuel and supplies at Midway and, at dusk, set out to sea again.

That night at supper Phil Carney asked the Skipper if they were going to start enemy-territory routine.

Stevenson thought for a moment and then said, "Not for a day or two, Phil. The patrol plane boys at Midway said they hadn't sighted any sign of Jap activity for a week or two. So we'll run on the surface during the day as well as the night. I want to get out there and finish this job and get back so we can get ourselves back into the war."

"So do I, Skipper," Carney agreed. "But I'd hate to get back into the war by having some Jap plane spot us on the surface in daylight and knock our ears off."

Stevenson laughed dryly. "So would I. In order to avoid that, I've written in the night order book to ride the vents at dawn."

"That'd help," Carney agreed.

"I have also instructed the daytime lookouts and the radar watch to be on their toes. If they do their jobs properly they should be able to spot a plane in plenty of time for us to get under and out of the way."

"Those things come in pretty fast, sir," Carney said dubiously. "And we still aren't diving as fast as we should be."

"Maybe being west of Midway will speed the boys up a little. Maybe the sight of a Jap plane with that tomato ketchup spot on it will hurry 'em up, huh?"

"I hope we don't have to have that," Carney said.

"It's safe as a church. Remember when the Japs tried to take Midway we whaled the daylights out of them. They won't be back for a long time."

"They still own the rest of the Pacific," Carney said. "They've got a lot of island bases to keep supplied. That'll mean a lot of planes and ships moving around out here."

"I've already told you that no Jap movement has been sighted for a week or so. I'm in a *hurry*, Phil. I want to get this job done and over with. I see no reason to spend all day submerged. It's hard on the crew, hard on the batteries, and it's slow."

Ken watched Carney's face as he said, "Yes, sir." Carney's eyes were sober and worried. He was not happy.

After Ken, Si, and Pat got into bed, Ken asked, "What was that discussion at supper all about?"

Si answered from his bottom bunk. "Generally, after we leave Midway and get out into enemy water we go submerged during the day and only come up to charge batteries during darkness. But the Skipper wants to run on the surface for a couple more days."

"And Carney doesn't want to?" Ken asked.

"I don't blame him," Si said. "You're kind of asking for it to be caught on top during daylight."

Malone said angrily, "And I said last night that he was scared. Now I don't know whether he's scared or just dumb. He's never seen how fast a Jap plane can come right out of the sun and blast you. I hear that our fly-boys in the Atlantic are giving the Nazi subs a beating. Just blowing 'em out of the water. Remember that joker who said, 'Sighted sub, sank same'? He was a fly-boy who got a Nazi on the surface in daylight."

Si said seriously, "The crew isn't going to like this one little bit, Pat."

"I know it. I'll bet Willy has already told them every word the Skipper and Phil said. I can just hear the guys up in forward torpedo or maneuvering hashing it over. They've got a Skipper who's not only scared but stupid, too."

"Take it easy, Pat," Si said. "He could be right, you know. He might have gotten some dope at Midway he hasn't told us about. There might not be any Japs within a thousand miles of here and he knows it."

"I sure *hope* so," Malone said.

"What does riding the vents mean?" Ken asked.

Si said, "Usually when we're on the surface the valves and vents to the ballast tanks are closed. You see, the water comes in through what we call Kingston valves in the bottom of the boat and pushes the air out of the tanks through the vents. Now when you ride the vents you open the bottom valves but keep the vents closed. The water can't get into the tanks against the air pressure that way. Then if you have to dive in a hurry, all you do is open the vents. It saves a few seconds getting under the water."

"Oh," Ken said. "One more question. I guess from now on we'll be doing crash dives?"

Malone laughed. "I don't know where those movie characters got that expression 'crash dive.' There just ain't no such animal. Every dive in a boat is a crash dive. You do every one of 'em just as fast as you can. If the Skipper of a boat started hollering 'Crash dive!' the way they do in the movies the crew wouldn't know what he was talking about."

"We never say anything but 'Dive' or 'Take her down,' something like that," Si added.

"I had a Skipper who made it a point never to seem excited about *anything*," Malone told them. "So we always knew when he was excited. When nothing was going on he'd order 'Dive the boat' just like anyone else. Now if anything *was* going on, he'd be calm as milk and say, 'Well, boys, let's go downstairs.'"

"I've noticed that the Skipper isn't the last man to come down off the bridge," Ken observed. "I thought that was an old Navy tradition."

"Not in the boats, Ken. The Skipper's got to get below to the conning tower. The last man off the bridge is always the Quartermaster, and it's his job to close the hatch. So he gets to step on everybody else's fingers going down the ladder but nobody ever steps on his. I knew a Quartermaster who just loved to jump down right on

79

my head. I wore a helmet every time I had a watch with that guy."

"If I ever learn this Japanese and get some spare time I'm going to try to find out what goes on in this boat," Ken told them.

"Don't," Pat advised. "It'll drive you batty. Just look at the instructions for flushing the toilet."

Ken laughed, remembering those instructions.

This is how you flush a toilet in a submarine:

1. Close bowl Flapper Discharge Valve A.
2. Open Gate Valve C in discharge pipeline.
3. Open Valve D in water supply line.
4. Open Valve E.
5. Close Valve D.
6. Close Valve E.
7. After use, pull Lever A.
8. Release Lever A.
9. Open Valve G in air supply line.
10. Rock Valve F until pressure is 10 pounds above sea pressure.
11. Open Valve B.
12. Rock valve lever inboard to blow overboard.
13. Close Valve B.
14. Close Valve C.
15. Close Valve G.

CHAPTER 6

Mu'ti-ny, *v.i.* . . . . To rise against, or refuse to obey,
lawful authority in military or naval
service.

Ken closed the dictionary and stared straight down the
empty wardroom. In the bookshelf he saw the familiar
canvas straps and metal binder of the book of Navy Regulations.

Putting the dictionary back, he got the Regulations
and ran his finger down the index under M. Munitions,
Murder, Muster, Mutiny.

Mutiny was sub-paragraph (1) under Article 4: Of-
fenses Punishable by Death.

He closed the book without reading it.

At eight o'clock that morning he had gone once more
to see Stevenson. He had pointed out to him that, while
the op plan might look good on paper, it actually was
impossible to accomplish. He had reminded Stevenson of
the admiral's warning that it was imperative to keep the
Japanese from suspecting that their radio station had
been discovered.

Stevenson had been surprisingly pleasant and patient,
so Ken, his hopes rising, had said that the only way was
for the boat to come in close to the islands at night to
let him out. Then come back in close to pick him up before dawn. That, he had insisted, was the only way,
unless, of course, Stevenson would take the boat into the
lagoon.

Stevenson, his voice pleasant, had said, "Mr. Braden,

you will execute the operation plan as approved by me." Then he had added, "That is a command."

Would it be mutiny? Ken wondered. If he could, somehow, get this op plan to the admiral and let him see how suicidal it was not only as a threat to Ken's life but as a threat to the success of the mission—would the admiral consider his refusal mutiny?

He wasn't sure, but he was fairly sure that Stevenson would try to have him court-martialed. It would certainly be the end of his career in the Navy.

What would his father think? Ken wondered. His father, an Army doctor, had devoted his life to military service and he had great pride in the Armed Forces of America. If he was now still alive in some Japanese prison camp how would he feel when he heard that his son had disgraced himself and been dismissed from the Navy?

At last, as the *Shark* rammed her way eastward on the surface, Ken stripped the problem to the bare bones. If he tried to carry out the op plan as approved he would, inevitably, be caught in daylight on or near one of the islands. That was absolutely unavoidable. If he was seen by the Japanese they would know instantly why he was there.

That was one side of it. Now if he refused to carry out his orders, that would be insurrection, mutiny.

What should he do?

Ken got up, put the book of Regulations back on the shelf, and picked up his overseas cap. As he started to put it on he looked at the little gold eagle on one side of it and at the lone silver bar on the other.

They would take that eagle and that bar off his cap. They would take the thick and the thin gold stripe off the sleeves of his coat, and take the gold buttons off.

Ken put his cap on and stepped out into the corridor.

He had made his decision. He was not going to obey Stevenson's command.

There was no answer when he knocked at Stevenson's cabin.

Willy, coming by with a tray of clean coffee mugs, said, "I think he's back aft, sir."

"Thanks, Willy."

Passing the radio shack, Ken went into the control room. There was a feeling of alertness here. No one was talking, no one playing cards, or lounging around. There was a man on each of the big wheels which controlled the bow and stern planes; a chief was standing by the long levers which opened and shut the valves and vents; another chief was looking up at the panel of red and green lights glowing steadily above him.

"Seen the Skipper?" Ken asked a chief.

The chief jerked his thumb upward.

Ken, his mind concentrated on the words he was going to say, climbed slowly up the ladder to the conning tower.

There, too, men were alert, tense. The helmsman stared fixedly at the floating face of the compass warmly lighted in its bronze bowl as he slowly turned the spoked wheel a little to port, a little to starboard. The soundman, his headphones on, was listening to the probe of his radio waves going out through the water. The talker, odd-looking with the big sponge rubber pads over his ears, relayed the messages coming and going in a low, quick voice. Men on engine controls and enunciators stood in silence.

At the radar Pat Malone, the radar operator, and the Chief Electrician were talking almost in whispers.

"Seen the Skipper?" Ken asked.

"He's on the bridge."

Ken started for the vertical steel ladder which led up to the round hole between the deck of the bridge and the overhead of the conning tower. Then, with his foot on the ladder, he hesitated. "OK to go up?" he asked Pat.

Pat frowned. "He'll be down in a minute, Ken. You know how he hates unauthorized people on the bridge."

Ken went over and leaned against the bulkhead.

He needed a few more minutes, he decided.

He tried then to put into words what he was thinking. Careful, controlled words, for he knew that what he was going to say to Stevenson in a few minutes was going to have a profound effect on his future. The words he was going to use would be used again—against him—in his court-martial.

"Something ails our mechanical eye," Malone said over his shoulder.

"Turn it off," the chief told the operator.

In a moment Stevenson's voice came down from the bridge. "What's the matter with the radar? The antenna isn't moving."

Pat went over to the other end of the voice tube which went up to the bridge and said, "Radar's gone out, Captain. The chief's working on it."

"Bear a hand on it," Stevenson ordered. "This is no place to be running around blind, you know."

Then Ken heard Stevenson's order to the lookout float down through the open hatch. "Be alert, Ammons. The radar isn't working, so you're the eyes of the boat."

The lookout's voice sounded even fainter as he called down from his perch, "Aye, aye, sir."

"Here's the trouble," the chief said. "Just a bad tube."

"Good. Fix 'em up, will you, Chief?"

Pat went over to the voice tube. "Captain?"

Stevenson's voice came down flat through the tube. "Captain, aye, aye."

"Burned-out tube. Be fixed in a minute," Pat told him.

"Right. Check."

Ken heard Stevenson repeating the news to someone else.

The chief went over to the talker and said, "Tell Sampson to send me up a 6V6GT on the double."

The talker's voice, muffled in the shield around the phone's mouthpiece, said, "Juice, the chief wants a 6V6GT in conn. On the double."

Pat turned to Ken. "How's the boy?"

Ken looked at him and then away. "All right," he said.

Phil Carney came climbing down the ladder from the bridge. He nodded to Pat and Ken and went over to the radar. "Fixed yet?"

As the chief turned, a messenger came up from control with a new tube. "This what you want, Chief?"

"Yeah, thanks." He pulled the bad tube out, put in the new one, and turned the set on. The face of the radar was a dial-like glass with many concentric circles scribed on it. There were also thin lines radiating out from the center. Slowly the face turned a pale green. The chief flipped another switch, and a glowing white line running from the center of the tube to the outer rim began to revolve.

As the white line swept past east, a tiny spot near the outside of the dial glowed for an instant.

Ken heard Carney catch his breath even as he reached and turned a switch. The line swept around the dial faster, the white spot glowing again.

Carney did something and the line moved back and forth, only a little, the spot in the east growing brighter and moving in toward the center.

Ken remembered afterward, putting things together one by one, just about what happened then.

As Carney leaped to the voice tube to the bridge, Ken heard the lookout's voice in a sudden scream.

Carney said, "Bogey, Captain, bogey! Bearing one zero eight, distance five miles. Coming in fast. Aircraft." Then he whirled to the talker. "Rig out bow and stern planes."

The talker's voice sounded all through the boat. "Rig out bow and stern planes."

The lookout was still screaming, and Ken could hear his faraway, frightened voice clearly, crying, "Plane! It's a plane. It's a Jap!"

Then Stevenson's voice coming down through the open hatch. "Clear the bridge!"

Ken watched men come tumbling down through the hatch and down the ladder into the conning tower. Three of them were already down when he heard the sound. It was like the hard, rapid clapping of hands. Instantly after that he heard things striking the metal of the bridge with a ringing, hard *smack*.

Somebody on the bridge began to scream in agony.

In a moment Si Mount fell through the open hatch. He made no effort to catch the rungs of the ladder, but fell all the way to the steel deck.

Blood poured from somewhere under his clothes.

After Si came the Quartermaster, a young Irish boy named Murphy. Murphy stood on the ladder, his head up out of the hatch and yelled, "Bridge clear? Everybody down?"

There was no answer.

Murphy closed the hatch with a crash and spun the big wheel which locked it shut. "Hatch secured, sir."

When Murphy turned and climbed on down the ladder Ken saw that his face was concealed behind a mask of blood.

Now the machine gun bullets striking the superstructure had lost the clear, ringing sound. Even as Ken ran toward where Si lay on the deck, he listened to the hard cracking of the bullets against the steel. As he reached Si and knelt beside him he heard a different sound. This was heavier—like a huge hammer pounding on the side of the boat. It hit five times and then stopped.

Blood was coming from somewhere below Si's waist. As Ken unbuckled the belt and pulled the trousers down, he heard Stevenson say, "Dive the boat!"

The talker repeated the order, and all through the boat other orders and sounds began. The Klaxon hooted as the vents opened, the induction valves closed with a crash, the diesels stopped, and the motors began to whine.

Suddenly, in an electric voice, Carney said, *"Where's the Skipper?"*

Everyone in the conning tower stopped what he was doing and stared.

Carney leaped to the voice tube leading to the bridge. "Skipper? *Skipper?*" he yelled.

Stevenson's voice was a rough, strangled whisper coming through the tube. "I'm on the bridge. I'm hurt. Dive the boat, Phil."

Carney wheeled again. "Open that hatch! Get him down!"

Stevenson's voice sounded now cold, distant, and angry. "Mr. Carney, dive this boat. Take her *down*. The plane is coming in again and two more are following. *Take her down!*"

Carney said into the tube, "We're coming to get you."

The sound of the machine gun bullets began again, first into the water and then ringing against the steel.

A gasp and a choked-off moan came down through the tube. Then Stevenson, his voice very faint, said, "It's too late, Phil. I'm hit. Bad. Take her down, please."

Carney turned to the talker. His face was white, his lips gray, as he said, "Take her down."

The reports began to flash in.

"Green board."

"Air in the boat."

"Flood negative."

As the boat nosed under, Ken could hear the sea pouring over the foredeck. He could hear it rushing around the forward gun mount and then striking against the rounded steel of the tower.

Machine gun bullets were slamming into them again as the water rose.

Ken heard it gurgle as it struck the safety lines.

Then Stevenson's voice came for the last time. "So long," he said. "Good luck." They could all hear the voice tube on the bridge clang shut and then hear the water sweeping over the screen.

In a moment there was no longer any sound of the open water moving across the boat.

Carney stepped to the periscope. "Stop her at fifty-five, I want to take a look."

"Up periscope," he ordered, then stooped to his knees, waiting.

The oiled, metal shaft of the periscope began to move upward as motors somewhere hummed. As the handles snapped out when they cleared the edge of the well, Carney grabbed them and, rising as they rose, with his eye pressed against the rubber guard, he began to turn the scope.

The talker reported, "Fifty-five, sir."

"Very well," Carney said, swinging the scope aft. For a long, long time he held it steady there. Then he walked it slowly all the way around.

"Down periscope," Carney said, his voice quiet. He flipped the handles up so they wouldn't hit the well edge.

"Take her down to a hundred," Carney said. "All ahead full. Don't bother with silent running, they can't hear us anyway."

From below Ken could hear the orders to the bow and stern planesmen, and to the men on the ballast tank controls. In a moment the talker said, "One hundred feet, all ahead full."

"Put her on nine zero and hold her," Carney said.

The helmsman turned the wheel, the spokes slapping against his heads. "Course nine zero, sir."

Carney said to the people in the conning tower, "I think the Skipper's dead. I watched him for as long as I could see him. He was lying face down in the water. There was a lot of blood. He didn't move at all."

Then Carney went over to where Ken was working on Si.

Si had been shot in the leg, below the hip. Carney helped Ken put a belt tourniquet above the ugly wound and then turned to Murphy, who had by now wiped some of the blood off his face. Murphy's forehead had had the skin peeled back so that there was a loose flap of skin, but it didn't look very serious.

Carney said over his shoulder, "Go left to three six zero, hold it for one minute, and then go back to nine zero. All ahead standard."

"Aye, aye, sir."

Carney said to the talker, "Get the Pharmacist's Mate up here, please."

Carney patted Murphy on the shoulder. "You're going to survive, Murph, for many a St. Patrick's Day parade."

Then he turned back to Si, who was still unconscious from his fall. Where the bullet went in there was a bloody hole about the size of a fifty-cent piece, but, for some reason, the bullet had not exploded in him and had come out as neatly as it had gone in.

With the help of Pat, the stand-by helmsman, Ken, and the Pharmacist's Mate, they got Si down into the boat and stretched out on the wardroom table. Then Ken and Pat and the standby went back to get Murphy but he was already coming down the ladder by himself.

By the time they got back to Si the Pharmacist's Mate had cut away the rest of Si's trousers and was looking at the ugly, bloody wound.

Si came to and tried to sit up, but they pushed him back.

"Something's wrong with my leg," Si announced.

"It's got a hole in it," Pat told him. "Can you move it?"

Si moved it, wincing, then laid it down again.

"I don't think it hit the bone," the Pharmacist's Mate said. "I'm going to give you a shot, sir. Then all I can do is clean it up a little."

"That's the Navy for you," Si said. "When in doubt give all hands a shot."

The Pharmacist's Mate grinned as he snapped the end off the morphine Syrette. He jabbed the needle into Si's arm and said, "Now I'll work on Murphy until that takes effect on you, sir. What happened, Murph? Willy, you got any hot water?"

"Coming up," Willy said from the service pantry.

"How do you feel, Si?" Pat asked.

"Fine. I hurt all over. Who pushed me down the ladder?"

"I did, sir," Murphy said. "I'm sorry, but you were having a little trouble getting down."

"Thanks, Murph." Si looked up at Pat. "I don't hear any ash cans. What's happening?"

"We're zigzagging at a hundred feet. No depth charges yet."

"Maybe those planes didn't have any," Si said.

As the Pharmacist's Mate cleaned Murphy's head, Ken sat down on the table beside Si. "That stuff taking effect yet?"

"Some. I feel groggy. Boy, that plane got to us in a hurry, didn't it? Anybody else get hurt?"

Ken was about to tell him when the loud-speaker clicked and the talker's voice said, "Attention in the boat. Now hear this."

There was a pause and then Carney began to speak, clearly and slowly. "This is Carney, the Exec. Men, the commanding officer is dead, so I have assumed command of the boat until I get further orders.

"Now, for those of you who don't know what happened, I would like to tell you that the Skipper gave his life for us. He was hit by the first plane to attack and was not able to get off the bridge. He refused to let anyone open the hatch and go get him. Instead, he ordered the boat to go down before it could be torn open by the heavy-caliber machine guns." Carney stopped for a moment.

Then he went on. "I would like for all hands to join me in prayer. Oh Lord, we who are alive in this boat want to thank You for giving Paul Stevenson the courage he had. Now his body lies in the open sea, lost to all men, but his spirit of courage and self-sacrifice are not lost. God, be good to Paul. Amen."

CHAPTER 7

FOR A LONG TIME THERE WAS SILENCE in the wardroom. There seemed to be silence all through the boat. Ken could hear only the pulse and whine of motors, the sound of air coming from the blowers. No man made a sound.

At last Si Mount asked, "What happened, Ken?"

Ken looked down at him. The morphine had already taken effect and his eyes were glazed and sleepy-looking, his words slow and indistinct. "Nothing, Si. Go to sleep."

"Yeah. Sleep," Si said, closing his eyes.

By this time the blood had been washed off Murphy's face. Ken saw him slowly raise one hand to his eyes and then let it fall back into his lap. "It was my fault," he said, whispering. "I left him up there."

"No, it wasn't, Murph," Pat said, sitting down beside him. "You couldn't see anything through all that blood. And I heard you asking if there was anybody up there before you closed the hatch. It wasn't your fault or anyone else's, Murph."

"I thought the Skipper went below with the first ones to go," Murphy said in a low voice. "I didn't even know he was wounded."

"Nobody did."

Murphy began to cry. "It's my job to see that the bridge is cleared before I close the hatch. It's my *job!*"

The Pharmacist's Mate said quietly, "The morphine's getting to him, Mr. Malone. He'll be asleep soon."

As Murphy put his head down, the loud-speaker

clicked and Carney said, "All officers report to the conning tower."

As Pat and Ken walked aft, Pat said slowly, "I wish there was some way I could take back the things I said about the Skipper. I wish there was some way I could apologize to him and tell him that he was a brave man."

"I do, too," Ken said. "What he did took all the guts in the world."

When they climbed up into the conning tower the place was crowded. There were not only the regular watchstanders but all the officers as well as the talker and the lookout who had been on the bridge.

The lookout was talking as Ken and Pat found a place to stand.

"Well, Mr. Carney, it wasn't long after the Skipper noticed that the radar antenna wasn't turning that I saw this black dot up in the sky. Oh, right after he noticed the radar had stopped he warned me to keep a sharp lookout.

"Anyway, I guess the plane was five miles away when I saw it. But it was already in its dive. It came right out of the sun so I didn't see it until it was on top of us. So I yelled that a plane was coming. So the Skipper said, 'Clear the bridge,' and I jumped down from the scope housing and went on down the hatch."

"Were you the first one down?" Carney asked.

"I was, sir," the talker said. "Right after the Skipper ordered the bridge cleared he pulled my phone jack out and pushed me toward the hatch. I went on down. I never did see the plane."

The lookout said, "It was a twin-engine bomber, sir."

Bill Adams, who had been on the bridge, said, "It looked to me like that new Mitsubishi with the 20-millimeter cannon in addition to the 50-caliber machine guns."

"They were shooting something heavier than 50's," Carney agreed.

Adams went on, "As the splashes came across the water I could see two or three that were much bigger than the others. Then, when they came up the deck and began to hit the screen and come into the bridge, I saw Si Mount get it. It knocked him all the way back against the searchlight. I went back there to get him and helped him to the hatch. The Quartermaster and I got him started down the ladder all right, but he slipped and fell. Then I went down."

"Where was the Skipper?"

"I don't know, sir. It sounds stupid now, but at the time I thought, considering how long it had taken me to go aft and bring Si to the hatch, that the Skipper would have had plenty of time to get off the bridge."

"That leaves only the Quartermaster," Carney said.

"He says it was his fault," Ken said. "But he says he didn't see the Skipper get hit and that when he, himself, got hit he thought he had been blinded. He couldn't have seen anything through the blood in his eyes anyway."

"It wasn't Murph's fault," Pat added.

"No. It wasn't anybody's fault. Where was he when you saw him last, Bill?"

"He was on the starboard side. He had gone aft to see what was wrong with the radar and he must have still been back there by himself when he got hit."

"Then he must have crawled or pulled himself forward to the voice tube," Carney decided. "Very well. That's all. I want the officers here for a moment."

As the conning tower cleared a little, the officers stood in silence around Carney.

Carney said, "Under Article 181 (b) of Navy Regs, I'm assuming command of the ship. Frank, you'll be the Exec. Bill, you'll have to take over as First Lieutenant until Si gets on his feet again. Ken, what do you know about communications?"

"Only what I learned in midshipman school, sir."

"Can you run a coding board?"

"A little."

"Good. The first thing to encode and send as soon as we get up is this:

COMMANDING OFFICER SHARK MISSING IN ACTION STOP PRESUMED DEAD STOP EXECUTIVE OFFICER ASSUMING COMMAND STOP MISSION NOT JEOPARDIZED STOP REQUEST INSTRUCTIONS STOP.

"Aye, aye, sir," Ken said, writing it down.

The Pharmacist's Mate stuck his head up through the hatch. "Skipper, Murphy's all right. But I don't know what to do for Mr. Mount. You think I ought to run a penicillin swab all the way through the hole in his leg, or just let it soak through?"

"Have you probed for broken or splintered bones?" Carney asked.

"Yes, sir. Can't find any."

Carney thought for a moment. "I don't believe it's a good idea to run a swab through. Put a lot of penicillin on each side and then give him a stiff shot of it."

"Aye, aye, sir."

Carney turned to Frank Doherty. "Why've we got such a list to starboard, Frank?"

Frank was about to answer when the telephone talker said, "Captain, the Chief of the Boat says he can't keep pressure on the starboard main ballast tank. Says it's full of water."

"Tell him to keep her level by filling tanks on the other side." Then Carney turned again to Frank. "What do you think?"

Doherty was frowning and pulling at his right ear. He looked over at the clock on the bulkhead and then at the inclinometer.

Carney said to the talker, "Ask the chief to recheck his valves and vents."

In a moment the talker said, "Chief reports all valves and vents shut tight, sir."

Carney turned to Doherty again. This time Doherty nodded his head.

"Must have been those 20-millimeter cannon," Carney said.

"I heard them hitting the boat," Doherty told him, "but I didn't hear any explosions afterward."

"Neither did I. They might have gone off on impact." Carney looked at the clock. "Eight more hours of daylight, at least."

Doherty nodded.

"With the main starboard tank full of water we can't keep her from sinking," Carney said.

"Maybe we could pump out all the other tanks and get enough buoyancy to keep her where she is," Doherty declared.

"That might roll her over, Frank. If the water here isn't too deep we can let her go to the bottom and sit it out until nightfall. Then bring her up to the surface and see what we can do about the holes. Sound, how deep is it here?"

The soundman flipped a switch and listened for a moment. Then he said slowly, "Fifteen thousand feet, Captain."

Doherty bit his lip.

"All right," Carney said. "The only way we can keep her from sinking all the way is to pull maximum power on all engines and maximum up-angle on the planes. The batteries won't take that for eight hours."

The depth gauge now read 130 feet.

Carney turned to the talker. "Tell all hands that we've got a hole in the boat. We're going upstairs. If those planes are still hanging around we'll have to fight 'em off with the deck guns. We can't stay down here any longer." Then he added, talking only to Doherty, "Or we'll be down here forever."

Doherty nodded.

As the talker repeated the message—his voice just a

murmur in the guarded mouthpiece—Carney went to a phone on the bulkhead. "Sparks? We've got to ram this boat up to the top. Give her all-ahead flank. Don't nurse it; give her all you can get."

"Surface!" Carney ordered.

The horn sent three blasts through the boat.

"Blow all ballast."

"All hands man your battle stations for surface action."

Carney watched the depth gauge as the sound of the electric motors became stronger and stronger until it was almost like a thousand people screaming.

The hand on the depth gauge began to move back toward the 100-foot mark. At the same time the deck began to tilt sharply to starboard.

Doherty said, "She's getting critical, Skipper."

"Let's don't roll her over, Frank. Let's see if she can twist herself out of it. Keep her ahead emergency on the starboard prop but try going astern for fifteen seconds on the port."

Ken could feel the wrenching pressure of the opposed screws as the red bubble slid back toward the center.

The depth gauge moved down to 90 feet.

"All ahead now," Carney ordered.

So they brought her up, twisting and rolling, and very slowly.

At sixty feet Carney put the periscope up and walked it all the way around. "Don't see anything, but they can be up there."

He kept searching with the scope as the boat went on up.

Ken then heard the water draining from the bridge and gushing out of the scuppers.

As she broke the surface a stream of men poured out of all hatches and ran to the guns. It took only seconds to man the two cannon, one on the foredeck and one aft, and to unlimber and load the two machine guns on the bridge.

The boat was lying on the surface with a hard list to starboard, so that half the deck was awash most of the time.

"Let's take a look, Frank," Carney said. "Ken, hold that dispatch to Pearl until we see how much damage they did."

Ken followed Doherty and Carney up the ladder and out on the bridge. Bill Adams had the deck and reported the radar screen clear of enemy aircraft.

Carney climbed down the outside ladder to the deck. Already the Chief of the Boat was there with a small group of men. "What a lashup," the chief said with disgust as Carney came over. "With the boat over on her side this way we can't find the hole. And there's no way to get the water out without closing that hole."

Carney nodded as a wave hit forward and sent water running around his legs. "How big a hole is it, Chief?"

The chief shrugged. "A 20-millimeter can do a lot of damage. Maybe they got two or three into us. She filled up in thirty seconds."

Doherty said, "We'd better head for Midway, Skipper."

"That long run on the surface isn't healthy," Carney said. "Anyway, I'd hate to come home with, maybe, only a couple of small holes in her." Then he said angrily, "I wish I *knew* how badly we're hurt."

"Let me take a look," Ken said.

Carney stared at him. "The hole's down there somewhere. Under water."

"I know. But if there isn't enough daylight—and I think there is—I've got a good underwater lamp."

"Ohhh," Carney said slowly. "The UDT stuff. Fine, Ken. Go ahead."

It didn't take Ken long to strip down to his skivvy pants and get the rebreather on. He was clumsy in it as he climbed out of the hatch and walked back to Carney.

Carney called up to the bridge, "Stop all engines. We're putting a man over the side."

Ken gave the chief one end of the life line and tied the other to his belt. "One yank means I'm OK. I'll yank it every now and then. Two means pull me up. But a lot ot them, coming fast, means pull me up in a hurry."

"Yes, sir," the chief said. "One, OK. Two, pull up. Three or more, heave away."

Ken exhausted all the air from his lungs so as not to put any nitrogen in the rebreather, then he clamped the face mask on and opened the valve of the oxygen tank.

He heard the oxygen hissing into the canvas lung on his back and felt the lung fill up. Still standing on deck, he took a breath to check the gear.

Trailing the light nylon rope, Ken waded down the flooded deck, climbed over the sub's life line, and sank slowly into the water.

The Pacific was warm and the water very clear. He fended himself away from the rough side of the boat as the waves washed him back and forth.

He sank slowly down until he was below the scuppers. Then, in a systematic search, he moved forward and aft, going down a foot or so each time. It wasn't necessary to feel with his hands for he could clearly see the steel side of the boat.

He searched for half an hour without finding any break in the hull. Each time he went down deeper he would give one yank on the cord.

He knew that he was taking a long time and that Carney would be unhappy about it. After all, lying dead-still on the surface was an invitation to murder, but there was nothing else he could do. He had to keep on, slowly, looking at every inch of the dull steel in front of him.

He found, at last, three holes with ragged edges. To

make sure, he kept on searching past and below them, but there seemed to be only three of them.

On the way up Ken measured with how many lengths of his body it took before he reached the scuppers. As he waded out of the water and slipped the mask off he heard Carney yell up to the bridge, "All ahead standard."

Ken walked over to the group. "There are three holes about the size of my head, Skipper."

As the sub began to move through the water, Ken followed Carney and the rest back toward the bridge. On the way he told them how far down he estimated the holes were.

"Oh-oh," the chief said. "We couldn't get to them with a welding torch even if we were on an even keel, Captain. They must have hit us when we were rolling to port."

Carney just nodded as he stood looking ahead, his elbows on the splinter shield. Where the bullets had torn through it rust was already forming on the jagged edges.

Carney at last walked over to the open hatch and said, "Send up an area chart, please."

Ken took his gear off and waited, the sun feeling good on his bare skin.

"What are you planning to do, Skipper?" Doherty asked. "Take her back to Midway or Pearl?"

"I don't know," Carney told him. "Those planes know we're out here and they know just about where we are. They might also know that they rang the bell on us. There must have been a lot of bubbles of air coming up through those holes after we went down, and even after we got under way. My guess is that they've gone for help. Or to load up with depth charges."

Doherty looked at his watch. "Six, six and a half more hours of daylight."

Carney nodded. "It shouldn't take them more than

three or four hours to get back here from Kwajalein. It would take destroyers until tomorrow morning."

"Maybe if we poured the coal to her we could get away from them."

Carney thought that over, but shook his head. "The Japs aren't dumb, Frank. They'd figure that either one of two things happened. First, if they don't see us around where they hurt us, they'll figure they either sank us or that we're damaged but still able to move. If we can move, they'll figure we've headed for Midway because it's so much closer than Pearl."

A messenger came up the hatch with a chart.

Carney unrolled it on the small shelf on the bridge and, for a long time, studied it, occasionally taking measurements.

At last he spoke again, "They'll keep a search plane on our route to Midway, Frank, so that's out."

Doherty said helplessly, "What's *in*, Skipper?"

Carney reached for the phone. "Pat? Here's a detail for you. Call a working party together. Tear some cork off the overhead—rip out a good deal of it. Then get about a barrel of oil; good, black, used oil will do fine. Then I want everything that'll float—life preservers, mattresses, clothing—anything we can spare. And an air flask. Put enough weight on it to sink it."

He hung up the phone and turned to Bill Adams. "Take us back to where they hit us, Bill."

As the submarine turned and headed back, Pat and his working party began shoving stuff up out of the forward hatch.

After a few minutes the lookout called down, "Sharks, dead ahead, Captain."

"Very well," Carney said. He lifted his binoculars and looked for a long time at the dark blue water ahead of the boat. "All engines ahead one third," he said. "Put the boat in a slow circle, Bill."

101

Now Ken also could see the fins of sharks slicing through the water.

Moving slowly, the boat swung in a wide circle until it came back into its own wake.

Carney said slowly, "He's gone. I only hope he was dead before the sharks got to him. All engines stop."

"All right," Carney called down, "dump that stuff overboard."

The working party on deck threw over some mattresses, the drum of oil, slabs of cork, some life jackets, and a box of empty milk tins which floated tipped over.

Carney went down on deck as the air flask appeared from the hatch. "Just crack the valve," he ordered. "All we want is a stream of bubbles."

The weighted flask was lugged across the deck and dropped into the water. As it sank out of sight the silvery bubbles came steadily up and broke at the surface.

Carney stood for a moment looking at the trash floating in the water around the boat. "If I was a fly-boy I'd claim to have sunk a sub right here," he declared. Then he called up to the bridge, "All-ahead emergency. Course two eight zero. When you get a chance, Bill, drop down to the engine room and encourage the boys to keep those diesels rolling."

Ken suddenly remembered the message he was supposed to encode and send. He asked Carney about it.

"Nope. Hold it. No use giving those planes a fix on us by breaking radio silence now. Pearl will just have to wait."

"Where are we going, Skipper?" Doherty asked.

"Not to Midway, Frank," Carney told him. "Come on. I'll show you."

CHAPTER 8

THE FOUR BIG DIESELS WENT TO WORK. The exhaust gases burst from the stern of the *Shark* as she rammed forward, swinging to the new course.

By letting sea water into tanks on the port side they got the boat on a more even keel, although deep in the water and sluggish.

Phil Carney on the bridge glanced up at the sun in the absolutely cloudless sky. "Let's put a couple of lookouts out here, Frank," he suggested. "And let's keep the guns manned and ready. What about having them stand by both bow and stern torpedo tubes, too? If we get caught we'll just have to fight it out on the surface."

Doherty said, "Aye, aye, Skipper," and then gave orders to double the lookouts and to stay at battle stations. Into the phone he said, "Stand by all tubes. No target in sight, but we may have to shoot."

Carney went back to studying the chart. "The only way we can patch this boat is to beach her, Frank," he said at last. "Put her on the ground at high tide, patch those holes at low tide, and float her off on the next high."

Doherty nodded, but looked doubtful.

"Even beached she's going to be low in the water," Carney went on. "So we can't do any welding if there's any wave motion. We've got to keep it dry."

Doherty nodded again.

"See this?" Carney asked, pointing to the chart.

Ken looked too. Carney was pointing with the tips of his dividers at an island named Eugalin. "That bay looks deep and perfect. The bottom is sand, it's got a deep-water entrance and, inside the bay, the surface should be calm as a pond. We'll nose her into here, and then let her more or less drift aground. High tide is at four in the morning, which will be perfect if we can get there in time."

"How about Japs on the island, Skipper?"

Carney shrugged. "That's what I don't know. I've been trying to remember but I've never heard of any enemy activity on Eugalin. In the book it's just listed by name and nationality, but there's no mention of whether it's inhabited or not. And I can't remember anything in the news about the Japs taking it over."

"They might have—without saying anything about it," Frank argued.

Carney nodded. Then he looked forward at the sea rushing toward the bow of the boat and breaking in clean white waves which foamed all the way back to the conning tower structure. Finally he said, "Do you think a plane can get much of a radio bearing on us if we open up for just a few seconds?"

Doherty thought it over and then said, "They'd have to be shot with luck, Skipper. They'd have to be right on top of the frequency and have a direction finder beamed right on us to do them any good. Of course, if the transmission went on too long they could nail us."

Carney reached for the phone. "Communications? Who's this? Oh, Shelton. How long would it take you to send a dispatch to Pearl with a four-word message?"

Carney listened, then hung up. "Shelton says he could get it out in less than fifteen seconds, provided Pearl is on the ball—which he doubts."

"They couldn't get a bearing in that time," Doherty decided.

"All right. Ken, encode and send this. Address it Action JICPOA—that's Joint Intelligence Center, Pacific

Ocean Area—message to read: ANY JAPS ON EUGA-
LIN."

Ken repeated the dispatch, then climbed down
through the hatch. On his way forward he met Pat
Malone in the control room. "What's up?" Pat asked.

"We're heading for an island."

Ken went on to the tiny radio shack, where a first class
petty officer was sitting, the headphones on. He pushed
aside one earphone as Ken asked him for the coding
board.

The radioman looked worried. "May I see your au-
thorization, sir?"

"I haven't got any. The Skipper just made me Communications Officer."

"I wish he'd written it down, sir."

Then the phone rang. Ken could hear Carney's voice
saying, "Shelton, from now on Lieutenant Braden is
the Com Officer. Help him all you can, will you?"

"Aye, aye, sir." The radioman grinned at Ken. "Just
a formality, sir. Just orders from headquarters."

"Sure."

The radioman opened the safe and got out the coding board and strips. "Where's it going, sir?"

"Pearl. Action JICPOA."

"You don't have to code that—I know it already."

Ken, trying hard to remember how to work a coding
board, began putting in the strips for date and time.
As he went on, more and more of the method came
back and soon he was getting the message broken down
into the proper groups.

"Here you go," he said. "I hope there aren't any gar-
bles in it."

The radioman took the penciled groups of letters
which now spelled nothing. Starting the transmitter, he
reached for the bug.

Ken watched with admiration as he sent the message.
He was so fast on the double key that it sounded like an

almost continuous sound. It took him less than ten seconds from start to finish.

As the radioman turned off the transmitter, he said, "I bet every radioman in Pearl is down on Waikiki watching the hula girls. They don't even know there's a war on."

Ken sat on the wastebasket while the radioman listened.

"Well, what do you know?" he said. "Pearl says stand by."

Ken called the bridge and told the Skipper what was happening.

"Here it comes," the radioman said, writing. In a little while he handed Ken some groups of letters.

Ken decoded the thing as fast as he could and, not bothering to paraphrase it, wrote it as it came out.

NO DEFINITE INFORMATION REGARDING JAPS CIVIL OR MILITARY ON EUGALIN STOP BEST GUESS IS NOT INHABITED STOP ADVISE APPROACH WITH CAUTION STOP.

Ken took it up to Carney on the bridge.

"Wonder who's doing the guessing," Carney said.

"When we get near the island why don't you let me go ashore and take a look?" Ken asked.

"Good idea. It'll have to be a quick look, though, because if we miss the tide we'll have to wait another twelve hours."

For the rest of the day the *Shark*, wounded and wallowing, steamed toward Eugalin Island.

At midnight Ken climbed back to the bridge. "I'm all set, Skipper," he told Carney.

A dim red light flowed on the chart while above them the sky was ablaze with stars. Carney picked up the dividers. "Eugalin should be showing up on the radar soon. I plan to approach on the surface, circle it once, and take a look. If we see lights, then we'll stand off and you can go in and find out who's there. If there aren't any lights I think I'll take her right into the bay and you can go ashore from there."

"Wouldn't you think, sir, that if there are people on the island they would have some sort of boats? And if they have boats that they'd keep 'em there in the bay?"

"That's logical, and the bay's the only place small boats could be sheltered."

"Then I'll search the whole bay front first."

"No boats—no people," Carney agreed. "Even if there are Japs—say, a garrison—they would still have a boat to fish from, or to use to go out to any ships bringing in supplies. Natives would, of course, have boats."

Ken looked at the shape of the bay on the chart. "If I could get ashore here," he pointed out, "I could walk the whole bay front and get back in the water over here. That'd save me having to go over the same ground twice."

"I'll see whether we can get in there. But here's a thing that worries me, Ken. Suppose, while you're ashore, we get jumped. We'll have to go to sea to fight. We'll have to pull out and—leave you."

"I'd thought of that, Skipper."

"Have you thought much past that, though?"

"Only this far. I won't need any underwater gear to get ashore and back in the dark. Just compass, fins and a mask. But, just in case, I thought I'd take along a lung. I could sink it near the beach and mark it. Then if you had to take the boat back to sea, you could come back when you got through. You could stop right here in the mouth of the bay and I could swim out to you. I'd swim out every midnight and look around until you showed up."

"Sounds good. Let's make it that way. If we have to leave you behind we'll come back as soon as we can. I'll put the boat right here." Carney pointed to the middle of the entrance to the bay. "That'll give you only about half a mile to swim. I'll be there at midnight and will

107

stay until an hour before dawn. I'll come every night for a week. Then if you don't show—well, I'll put a landing party ashore and try to find you."

Ken nodded.

Now the sea was breaking over the bow of the submarine in sudden waves. The water was pitch black except for the breaking waves, which glowed with pale, horrible color.

A voice close by said, "Bogey, Captain. Dead ahead."

Carney bent to the voice tube. "Is it moving?"

"No, sir. Big and stationary."

"Stand by to dive the boat. Lookout, do you see anything?"

The lookout above them swung his night glasses slowly back and forth. "I'm not sure, sir, but there seems to be a dark mass dead ahead."

"Must be Eugalin," Carney said. Then he bent to the tube again. "Sound, when we get into sixty feet of water start reporting, will you?"

"Sound, aye, aye. Report at sixty feet."

"I can see it now," Carney said, pointing.

As Ken peered into the darkness, at last, he, too, could see a darker place, a low-lying dark, broad line.

"I'll go get my gear," Ken said.

In his cabin he stripped off his clothes and got into a light suit which covered him ankles to throat. It was grayish in color and, although it had no cold-protection qualities, it would be almost invisible on a beach at night, and it would also protect him from sunburn if he had to be exposed during the daytime. Into a watertight canister he put a diving lung with cylinders, a gallon of drinking water, some C rations, some extra ammunition for the .38-caliber revolver, the wrist compass, and an extra mask. Closing the canister, he attached a light blue buoy line with, on the end, a plastic float which was shaped and colored like a dried coconut.

Ken lugged the canister up the hatch on the foredeck and then went aft to get his fins and mask.

Waiting on the bridge, he watched the island sliding slowly by on the port side. From the voice tube came the monotonous reporting of the soundman as he called out the depth. Frank Doherty was now on the bridge with Carney and they both studied the island with their night glasses.

"That clump there looks like houses to me, Frank."

"Me, too. But I don't see any lights anywhere."

"No. You all set, Ken?"

"All set, Skipper."

Carney glanced at him in the dim red glow. "Wow! You look like an 1890 bathing beauty. Where'd you get the fancy long johns?"

Ken glanced down at the suit. The red light made it look exactly like old-fashioned red flannels.

They could now see the entrance to the bay.

"Let's nose in there," Carney said. "All engines ahead one third. Come left to nine zero and hold it."

"All ahead one third."

"On course nine zero."

"Let's be heads up on the guns, gents," Carney said. "The bushes might be full of 'em."

Shadowy figures down on the deck stood motionless at the guns while the machine gunners on the bridge swung their pieces slowly back and forth.

Ahead now they could see the long gray curve of the beach like a knife cut between the dark of the island and the dark of the sea.

"All right, Ken," Carney said. "This is your stop, I believe."

"Hollywood and Vine—all out," Doherty said.

"All engines stop."

Slowly movement of the submarine ended and it lay in the water quietly, with only a tiny lapping of the bay's gentle little waves against the ugly old hull.

"I'll wait right here for you until an hour before dawn —oh four hundred, Ken. If you're not back by then I'll have to pull out. But I'll be back at midnight tomorrow."

Ken nodded. "One other thing, Skipper. If there are Japs and it looks like they're going to get me, what can I do to let you know it won't be necessary to come back for me?"

"Take a Very's pistol and a flare," Doherty suggested.

Carney thought that over and then said, "There's no use telling the Japs how you got there, Ken. Isn't there some other way?"

"I think this'll work," Ken told him. "I'll drop the canister right here. Then if I get back tonight I'll pick it up. But if the Japs get me it'll still be here, so you'll know."

"Good."

Down on the foredeck Ken dropped the canister over the side. The plastic coconut floated low in the water and bumped hollowly against the sub.

As Carney said, "Good luck," Ken put on the fins and mask and slipped over the side.

The water was black, calm, and warm. Ken headed for the southern end of the bay and began to swim.

At the beach he lay in the quiet water and listened. He could hear the wind in the dry fronds of the coconut trees and he could hear the singing and squeaking of thousands of bugs and small animals. But there was no sound which he could identify as being made by man.

There were no footprints on the beach, nor any boats. Walking along in the shadows the starlight made under the trees, he went, stopping at every opening in the undergrowth to peer inland.

About halfway around the beach he finally made out a dark, foreign object lying under the palm trees. Taking the pistol out of the shoulder holster, he crept toward

110

it and, when he was near enough to see that it was a boat, hid behind a clump of bushes and studied it.

There was no movement, no man sound from the jungle. At last, creeping in the deep darkness, Ken got to the boat.

It was old and rotten. The bottom was gone and the ribs stabbed down into the sand.

Farther away from the beach there was a house in a little clearing. The floor was raised above the sand about two feet and the walls were of woven coconut leaf.

That, too, was old and deserted, the leaf walls rotting, gaps showing in the thatched roof.

Convinced now that the island was uninhabited, Ken nevertheless went on until he had covered the whole stretch of beach.

Swimming back, he soon saw the dark shape of the *Shark* lying low in the water. It had drifted a little so that he couldn't find the buoy marking where the canister was. But, he reasoned, it would be easy to pick it up in daylight.

Hands helped him over the life line and Carney asked, "What's the word?"

"I don't think there's a soul there," Ken told him. "There's one beat-up old boat and a falling-down house, but everything looks as though it was abandoned years ago. No footprints anywhere."

"Perfect. Bridge," Carney said, "all ahead one third."

"All ahead a third, sir."

Ken followed Carney back up the outboard ladder and explained about leaving the canister in the water.

The submarine began to move slowly ahead toward the long gray line of the beach.

Carney bent to the voice tube. "Frank, just keep steerageway on her. Close all bottom valves so we don't pick up a load of sand. And keep the depth reports coming."

The boat, barely moving, drew closer and closer to the island.

Carney said quietly, "We can get murdered in here. But I don't know what else to do."

Doherty came up through the hatch. "Five minutes to high tide, Skipper."

"All right. Hold her where she is. We want every inch of water we can get. Then, at four o'clock, ram her aground."

Doherty laughed nervously in the darkness. "I'm glad nobody in COMSUBPAC in Pearl heard that order, Skipper."

Carney chuckled. "It'd make good listening in a general court-martial, wouldn't it? And so the Skipper said, 'Ram her aground.'"

"You'd only get about twenty years in the Portsmouth Naval Prison."

Carney laughed out loud. "I'd almost swap those twenty years for these twelve hours coming up. Because we're going to be right here until tomorrow afternoon. All ahead full."

The diesels began to roar. The *Shark* drove forward through the water as the soundman chanted out the depths.

She hit hard and slid a little way up the beach.

"All stop."

There was a deep, still silence around the boat.

"Perfect," Carney said. "Now all we've got to do is wait for the tide to go out, patch her up, and we're on our merry way."

"Provided we can get off again," Doherty said.

Carney nodded. "Provided."

CHAPTER 9

THE MEN OF THE *Shark* WAITED for the sun to rise above the darkness of the Pacific. They knew that it would come suddenly with very little of that pre-dawn grayness which they were used to back in the States. The darkness, broken only by starlight and the faint light in the moving water along the hull, would simply disappear as the sun lunged up.

There wasn't much talking going on. Phil Carney, Frank, Pat, and Ken were on the bridge with the lookouts. Above them the radar antenna swung steadily, around and around, invisibly and silently searching for the enemy.

Down on deck the gun crews were standing by, dark shadows beside the long, greasy barrels of the guns. Farther along another group of men were waiting, standing beside the oxygen and acetylene tanks, one of them already wearing the welder's mask, pushed back high over his head.

Down inside the boat hardly anyone was still asleep. Willy was in the service pantry making sandwiches and coffee. In the crew's galley breakfast was on the stove. The men on watch worked, cleaning and repairing, adjusting and testing.

In the after torpedo room all bunks were empty of sleepers. The tubes were closed, the round, slightly bulged steel doors polished until they glittered. A man stood by each tube, the manual-firing lanyard in his hand in case the electric-firing mechanism failed. Overhead the torpedo loading tracks were cleared, the chains and hoists ready to swing new torpedoes from the racks along the walls of the compartment and on into the tubes.

The only machines running were the spare generators, the blowers, and the cooling pumps, so that the boat was unusually quiet.

Willy took some coffee and sandwiches into Si Mount's stateroom. By now the effects of the morphine had worn off and Si's wound was hurting him a good deal.

Then Pat Malone squeezed into the room past Willy and looked down at Si. "How's the boy?"

"I hurt."

"That's a fine attitude," Pat told him. "Here you are with a brand-new hole in you and you're complaining about it." He took one of Si's sandwiches and began eating. "You've got the Purple Heart, man!"

"That's a medal I could do without," Si told him. "What's the word, Pat? The last thing I remember the plane was strafing us."

Pat sat down carefully on the edge of the bunk and told him what had happened.

At the end Si said, "If they spot us we're finished."

Pat nodded.

Si laughed and then winced. "And they told us this was just going to be a joy ride."

At last the water of the bay sank low enough to expose the holes in the side of the *Shark*. The silence which had been so heavy in the boat was instantly broken. Machinists with heavy hammers attacked the ragged edges of the holes. An electric grinder roared and screamed. Other machinists sawed and shaped steel plates for the welder.

On the bridge Carney gazed nervously at the silent green jungle and then out across the bay and on out toward the rolling Pacific. The ear-splitting din rose up in clouds from the deck.

"I bet you can hear this racket for fifty miles," Carney said to Ken.

Ken, too, looked at the green, silent island. Only birds moved, some of them skipping along the beach, others sitting in the palm trees screaming warning signals into the jungle.

With the sun high in the sky there were no longer the shadows of the trees flowing out into the water. Ken put on his mask and fins and swam out into the bay looking for the plastic coconut.

The water was beautiful to swim in—clear and warm. He could see the canister when he was still yards away from it.

By the time he got back to the *Shark* the hammering and grinding had stopped, and the men were now rigging a framework out over the side. Using bed springs and rope, they covered the whole thing with mattresses, making a crude tent which would keep the flash of the welder's arc from being seen from the sky.

Ken put his gear away and got dressed. In the cabin with Si he drank some coffee and talked.

"It's already eleven o'clock," Si complained. "How long is it going to take those monkeys?"

"Doesn't much matter," Ken told him. "We can't get off the ground until high tide lifts us off, and that'll be after four."

Si swore. "I'm getting out of this sack. If I'm going to get my ears knocked off I want to be on my feet."

Ken laughed and, when Si tried to get up, pushed him back against the pillow. "Your leg is doing fine now. If you get up and walk around it'll get worse, and that just means trouble for all hands."

Si relaxed. "Six more hours. I'll be an old man by then."

Ken finished dressing. As he started out, Si said, "Listen, if anything happens give me the word, will you? I don't like lying here and not knowing what's going on."

"Every hour on the hour," Ken told him.

Back on the bridge he found Carney and Pat Malone studying the area chart.

"There're Japs here," Carney said, pointing to an island on the chart. "And here, too. There used to be a lot of shipping into this island before the war so there are probably docks of some sort."

Pat measured off the distance with the dividers. "Eighty miles, Skipper."

Carney played his finger tips on the bridge rail. Then he leaned over and called down, "How you coming, Chief?"

The chief looked up. "Only a few more minutes now, Skipper. You can start pumps now, if you want to."

Carney nodded and turned to the voice tube.

Soon the tent of mattresses was taken in and the welders swung back on deck. Doherty came out of the forehatch and inspected the plates which had been welded over the holes. Then he walked aft to the bridge. "They look all right, Skipper. Want to try 'em?"

"Let's don't take a chance on sand, Frank. See if you can pump her empty into the other tanks."

"Yes, sir."

Soon Ken heard the sound of pumps starting inside the boat.

As they waited, Pat said, "If there's no leak are you going to try to get her off the beach now, Skipper?"

"I'm going to try but I don't think it's going to work, Pat."

In a moment Doherty's head appeared in the hatch at their feet. He was grinning. "Tight as a drum, Skipper. I put as much overload on her as I could get out of the pumps but the needle stayed steady. I think she's as strong as she ever was."

Carney blew a breath of air up past his nose and smiled. "Good work. Tell Newman and Jones I'm proud of them. Best welders in the fleet. Now, Frank, what do you say we try to get off this beach?"

"I don't think she's going to come off before high tide, Skipper. If then."

"Neither do I, but do you think it's worth trying?"

Doherty thought for a moment. "We might do this. Pump everything out of one valve. Then maybe Ken could go down there and see that we haven't jammed anything into the valve. I can see some good-sized sea shells down on the bottom and it wouldn't take but one jammed in the valve seat to take care of us but good."

"Is that feasible, Ken?" Carney asked.

"Easy. I can do it standing on my head. In fact, that's the only way I can do it."

Ken went below and got a rebreather since he was used to them and wasn't yet sure about the new Aqua-Lung they had sent him.

By the time he got the absorption cylinder in and the oxygen bottle hooked up, Doherty had pumped all the water out of the boat.

On deck Carney showed him just about where he could find the valve and, carrying a towel, Ken went over the side.

He found the opening without any trouble at all, and found, also, only a thin coating of sand on the valve seat. He wiped this off with the towel and then hammered on the boat.

Keeping out of the way, he stayed down there as the valve slowly closed.

Back on deck Carney helped him out of the rebreather and said seriously, "I think every sub ought to have one of these outfits, Ken, and a man who knows how to use it. There's a lot of times when a skipper would give his right arm to know what's going on below the water line. What does it take to learn how to use a lung like that?"

"Not much, Skipper. At first you panic. Everybody

117

does. That's why you always go down first with someone else. Then, when you get over panicking, there's nothing to it—at medium depths anyway."

"What happens when you go deep?" Carney asked, walking back toward the bridge.

"That's something psychological that they don't know much about yet. I've never felt it but they thought back at school that a few of the deaths were caused by it. The guys I've talked to who have felt it say that it's a kind of happiness. You get so happy down there you forget what you're doing and where you are. You forget to watch your air supply and everything else. They say it's a wonderful feeling; like nothing else they ever felt. But it's dangerous."

"But that's only down deep?" Carney asked.

"Below a hundred and fifty feet."

"How deep can you go?"

"I don't know, Skipper. One man at school went a long way. We don't know how far he actually went because he never came up again. But he was alive and able to communicate all right when he reached four hundred feet."

"*Four hundred!*" Carney said, whistling. "The pressure of the sea would flatten this boat at four hundred feet. At least, I'm not going to take her down that far to find out what would happen. I've been in a boat at three hundred and she screamed in every joint."

On the bridge Carney began giving orders to start engines and try to back off the beach.

As the diesels began to throb, Carney called, "All back full. Maximum power."

The whole boat trembled and shook as the gushers of sandy water flowed around her stern and poured forward toward the shore. Pat Malone kept his eye on the beach.

The *Shark* didn't move.

"All engines stop," Carney ordered.

"There's not enough water to float her," Doherty decided. "Nothing to do but wait."

Over the loud-speaker system a boatswain's pipe shrilled and then the sad voice called, "Reee-lieve the watch."

As men came out of the forward and after hatches to relieve the men on the guns and lookout stations, Carney turned toward the hatch. "I'm hungry," he announced.

Pat Malone was folding up the chart. Frank Doherty was talking over the bridge rail to a man on deck. Two lookouts who had been relieved were climbing down the outboard ladder of the bridge. Ken was waiting for Carney to get clear of the hatch before he, too, went below. The whole crew of the forward gun suddenly started laughing.

The man watching the pale green face of the radar said, "Bogey, Captain."

Carney's reaction was instantaneous. He turned loose the ladder rung and dropped the rest of the way down into the conning tower.

"Bearing one eight seven, distance nineteen miles, coming in fast. A plane."

"Any IFF?" Carney asked.

"Not yet, Captain."

Carney turned to the talker. "Sound GQ. Heads up on the guns."

As the gong began to beat, Carney went fast back up the ladder to the open bridge. He grabbed the binoculars and, without bothering to wrap the strap around his wrist, began peering at the southern sky. "Plane coming over," he said to the lookouts. "About one eighty at fifteen miles."

Then he said to the men on the machine guns, "If this is an enemy—and I think he is—knock him down. We don't want any more holes in the boat."

119

A gunner grinned and said, "Knock him down, aye, aye."

"Bearing still one eight seven, distance twelve," radar said.

Pat Malone had unfolded the chart again. "Puts him right over the island, sir."

Carney nodded.

"Want to try to get her moving again, Skipper?" Doherty asked.

"We've got a good, steady platform for the guns now, Frank. Let's keep it."

"When do you want to start firing?" Pat asked.

Carney tapped his finger tips on the rail. "If he's high and on his way, he might not see us. Let's wait and see what he does."

With the sun now straight up above him the sky looked deep blue and empty to Ken. The water of the perfectly calm bay, however, now had the look of old, tarnished brass.

There wasn't a sound on deck. Below there was the murmur of the generators and blowers, and there was a faint squeak as the radar antenna turned, now slowly, just back and forth a few degrees.

"Bearing still one eight seven, distance eight, altitude twelve thousand."

Then, faintly, they could hear the sound of the plane. It came drifting down to them from the deep blue sky and whispered around them as they stood, every man looking up.

The sound of the plane grew stronger and stronger and, at last, Carney said, "There he is," and pointed.

It was only a dot, a speck, in the sky. It seemed to Ken to be motionless up there.

Now a hammering noise came down on them from the sky. Carney turned to the talker and said, "Tell radio to ride the Japanese military plane frequency."

In a moment the talker said, "Radio says he's been on it for five minutes. He doesn't hear anything."

Carney just nodded and went on studying the plane now passing high above them. It was still just a dot high in the empty blueness.

In a moment the talker said, "Radio reports that something has opened up. Seems to be calling 'Inoshi,' at least that's the only word that sounds like it's being repeated."

"Inoshi?" Ken asked. "Isn't that a Japanese destroyer class?"

"You're right," Carney said. "How about it, Pat?"

Pat, still measuring on the chart, said, "Yeah. And I think we can expect company about quarter past four, Skipper."

Carney looked at the chart. "Eighty miles," he said slowly, "twenty knots. It's going to be company all right if the Inoshi is there." He jabbed at the chart.

"We're going to get some right now," Pat said. "He's turning around."

Radar said, "Bogey turning, Captain."

Carney looked up into the sky. "Well," he said quietly, "here we go again."

CHAPTER 10

AGAIN THE SOFT HAMMERING of the plane's engines floated down from the sky.

Carney picked up the binoculars, found the plane and studied it for a few seconds.

The voice of the radarman began to drone. "Turning three zero. Turning six zero. Turning seven five. Turning nine zero. Turning one twenty. Turning one eighty. Steadying."

Carney said, "Give me range and bearing when you can."

Radar said, "Steady on course zero zero seven. Range twenty thousand. Altitude ten."

"He's down a little," Carney said. Then he reached for the microphone.

His voice through the loud-speakers sounded friendly and close. "Now hear this in the gun crews. That plane is coming back. I want some real old-fashioned Kentucky squirrel-shooting."

The muzzles of the deck guns swung around to starboard while the loading crew got ready, men standing in line from the gun to the hatch to pass ammunition. Up on the flying bridge the long snouts of the machine guns were moving very slowly downward.

Radar said, "He's coming straight in. Range fourteen. Altitude five."

"That's what I want," a man on the 20-millimeter gun said. "I want him coming right straight at me. I want him right down low."

Carney picked up the microphone again. "To the gun

122

crew that gets him there's going to be a steak dinner with all the trimmings at P. Y. Chong's."

The man on the 40 said, "I'm eating that steak."

Radar said, "On course. Range ten. Altitude one thousand."

Doherty said, "It's going to be low level. Maybe a skip bombing. Or torpedo."

Carney said into the microphone, "Fives, open on him at five thousand. Twenties and forties, hold your fire until he's in to two thousand."

The man on the 40 swore under his breath. "I won't get a chance at him."

Radar said, "On course. Range six. Altitude zero. He's right down on the deck. I can hardly read him."

Carney said in the microphone, "Stand by on the 5's."

Ken watched the plane coming straight at them. It was like a heavy black pencil line in the sky, with the engines and fuselage black dots in the line.

A voice on the deck bawled, "Open fire!"

As the 5-inch cannon began to fire, Ken could feel the boat shaking under his feet. They fired rhythmically, gouts of smoke bursting from the muzzles and floating back to shroud the gun crews loading the shells. The report of the guns was an enormous CRACK-WHANG, which deafened Ken enough so that the sound of the empty brass cases falling and rolling on the deck was only a tinkling noise.

Radar said, "On course. Range three. Altitude zero."

Ken looked out across the calm, peaceful, blue water at the plane sweeping toward him. A part of his mind said, *This is war. This is death.* But it all seemed unreal to him. He could not make himself believe that there were men in that airplane who *wanted* to kill him. It seemed so impersonal, so harmless. The shells of the deck guns were invisible in their flight and they touched nothing.

The plane was right down on the water and coming very fast. When it was only a mile away Ken could see the red Rising Sun painted on its wings and he could see the silver discs of the props and the glint of sunlight off the plexiglass dome. The glass across the pilot's cockpit was dark—like an empty window.

Ken heard Carney's voice. It sounded far away and, like the plane, unreal. "All right, gentlemen, let's see if you can show the 5's how to do it."

The 20 opened instantly with a furious deep-toned rattle, the bullets cracking out of the muzzle.

Ken watched the tracers sliding away, bright little balls of fire sliding straight away from him and toward the plane. He knew that between each of the tracers there were invisible bullets, but he couldn't *believe* it.

The wing guns on the plane began to fire. Ken watched the flickering at the muzzles—little bright flashes of light, regular little puffs of white smoke blown instantly away but left to hang behind the plane like footsteps.

But there wasn't a trace of a bullet. Ken could see nothing, hear nothing.

He turned his head and looked at the other people on the bridge. Pat Malone and Doherty were looking fixedly at the plane. The loaders for the machine guns were moving, carrying shells to the rattling, jumping, smoking guns. The men on the triggers were hunched over, their bodies shaking as though they were part of the gun they were firing. They, too, were sighting through the rings at the plane rushing toward them.

Only Carney wasn't looking at the plane. Ken watched him turn and look aft at the deck gun. Then he turned and looked forward at the other one. Finally he looked for a moment at the plane then at the 20-millimeter beside him. Carney's face was still, his eyes deep and thoughtful, his lips pursed a little.

The noise around Ken was monstrous. Beside him the 20 rattled and roared, the 40 kept up a steady, huge

POM POM POM while both the guns on deck CRACK-WHANGed. The air was thick with the smell of cordite and the smoke stung his eyes.

Radar said, "Range five hundred."

Ken looked down at the brass falling around his feet. The empties were flying out of the gun, bright and cheerful in the sunlight, then falling and bouncing on the deck, at last to lie still, little tendrils of smoke coming out of the pitch-black holes in them.

Mixed up in all the noise from the guns Ken began hearing another sound. It came down from just above his head. It was a high-pitched whistle broken by a sharp, hard SNAP. He looked up but saw nothing.

Then, suddenly, he realized that the sound was being made by the bullets from the plane. The SNAP was the shock wave striking him as the bullets went over.

He looked again into the calm, blue, empty sky and thought again, *This is war. This is death.*

Suddenly, as though a wave of the sea had swept over him and knocked him down, he was afraid. His knees began to shake and he had to hold on to the bridge rail to keep his legs from buckling and dumping him down with the empty brass.

Now, at last, he could see the two pilots in the plane. The dark window was no longer empty; there was now nothing unreal about this thing. There were two men in there with flight helmets on their heads and some sort of harness over their shoulders. They were sitting quite still, their dark faces looking toward him.

They were the enemy.

Carney was talking to the gunner on the 20. "Down a little, John. You're going over him."

Radar said, "He's all over the screen. He's too close."

Pat Malone said, "Hit him! *Hit* him!"

Carney said, "Here comes the bomb. You're right, Frank, he's skip-bombing it."

Ken watched the black bomb fall and hit the water. It was pretty to see—the black thing hitting the calm blue water and sending up a shower of bright, white, sparkling spray.

The bomb skidded like a flat stone, and then rose from the water and floated toward them for a moment in the air.

Ken didn't know it, but his mouth hung loosely open. He was holding to the bridge rail with both hands and his knees were knocking together.

The plane now seemed to be enormous and the flickering of its wing guns was close and an ugly bright, yellowish red.

The tracers were going just over the wings of the plane.

Carney said, "Down a little, John."

The lazy tracers began to float into the plane's wings. Ken watched the little bright balls shoot out of the muzzle, float toward the plane, and disappear into it as though absorbed.

The plexiglass dome of the plane went straight up into the air and hung there.

Then the glass windshield shattered and blew away. Ken, watching, saw the two pilots suddenly relax. They had been sitting up, bending forward a little—tense, intent. Now they sat back in their high seats and let their heads drop.

The port wing of the plane came off near the root and began to flop over in the air, the engine still running, the prop going slower and slower.

What was left swept on toward the bridge. Ken, standing straight up, watched it; watched the two men sitting as though asleep in the high-backed chairs. He kept bending his neck, his head going back and back as the plane went close over him—so close that he could see the bright-headed rivets along the bottom of the fuselage.

The 20 and 40 swung wildly around, following the sinking plane.

Down on the water the bomb still came, skipping along, making huge foamy footsteps toward them. It rose and floated, turning lazily over, then hit again and rose again.

It floated over the deck of the *Shark* so close that the gun crew ducked, then hit on the other side, rose and floated again, and landed in the jungle close beside the beach. Two palm trees rose straight up out of the ground and hung for a long time in the sky before they began to fall back into the ugly burst of sand and dirt flung up by the exploding bomb.

The plane hit the water with its wing tip and began to cartwheel. It rolled across the bay and then, suddenly, stopped. In a moment it sank.

Ken could hear people yelling and shouting but, to him, there seemed to be only a deep silence. Slowly he lowered his head and looked down at his knees.

He didn't think that the legs he saw were his. His trousers were shaking as though blown by a strong wind and inside the trousers the legs were hitting together.

Not believing this, Ken slowly reached down and touched the shaking legs.

They were his.

"The shakes," Carney said, standing beside him. "I get 'em every time."

Ken tried to grin while he also tried to make his legs stop shaking. "You know, this is my first time."

"That's always the worst one." Carney took a deep breath and blew it up past his nose. "That was too close."

Down on the foredeck the chief was striding up and down in front of his gun crew. He was swearing a blue streak. "Lousiest blank-blank gun shooting I ever saw. You let those blank-blank guys on the 20 beat me out of a steak dinner. You blank-blank swab handles are going to get gun drill every day for the rest of the trip. Blank blank blank."

Carney laughed a little. "That chief loves a steak," he said. Then he reached for the microphone. "Nice going, gents," he said. "But next time let's take him a little farther away. Now hear this, we're stuck here until about sixteen hundred. There may be another plane attack. Or there may be a destroyer in a few hours. Let's keep a heads-up detail on all guns and in the after torpedo room."

As he hung up the mike Willy stuck his head up through the hatch. "Chow down, Captain. We've got some nice fried chicken and I made some biscuits."

"All right, Willy. Be down in a minute."

Willy, whose head was about on the level with the empty brass of the machine guns, looked slowly around. "Taxpayers hurting today, boy. Man told me those bullets cost a dollar apiece."

One of the gun crew looked down at Willy's head. "Willy, you ever been to San Diego?"

"I been there," Willy said.

"You remember what that sign at the gate said?"

"What sign say what?"

The gun crewman stooped down so he was on Willy's level. "It said, 'It takes millions to win a war. To lose one—takes all you've got.'"

"Something to that," Willy admitted. "What was the shooting all about?"

"Oh, just a Jap plane."

"He get away?"

The crewman shook his head.

"I guess then the Jap taxpayers are hurting worse'n we are. Fried chicken real hot now, Captain."

"Coming," Carney said.

Willy looked once more at the gun crewman. "Who hit him?"

"Among others, I did."

128

"You getting better, boy," Willy decided, and disappeared down the hatch.

"Willy," Pat yelled after him, "how about bringing me up a piece of that chicken? I got the watch."

"You're a dark-meat man, aren't you, Mr. Malone?"

"That's right."

"And gravy on your biscuits?"

"That's right."

"Coming up," Willy said.

Ken followed Carney and Doherty down the ladder. In the wardroom they talked while they ate, going over the attack, each man remembering what he could of it.

As they sat around drinking coffee, Carney turned to Bill Adams, but before he could say anything, Bill grinned sheepishly and said, "I know, Skipper. That was mighty poor shooting. I'll see what I can do."

Carney smiled. "Thanks." Then he turned to Ken. "We've got about three more hours, Ken. How'd you like to take a look at that plane? There's a chance that you could pick up some gadgets Intelligence would like to see. Maybe even some code books."

"Don't you think the Japs do the same way we do?" Doherty asked. "Whenever one of our planes goes into the drink there's a gismo on it that blows up the radar, IFF, and all codes and charts."

"They might have," Carney admitted. "But since this one is in such shallow water it wouldn't hurt to give it a once-over-lightly, anyway. If you want to, Ken?"

"Very much," Ken said. "It'll give me a chance to try out the new breathing gear they sent me, too."

Ken spent almost an hour reading the instructions for the Aqua-Lung and studying the whole rig until he was sure he knew how to use it.

At two o'clock he and Pat Malone set out in the rubber boat, looking for the plane. In the shallow, clear water it was easy to spot.

Ken put on his mask and fins and slipped overboard.

He liked the Aqua-Lung immediately. He found that it was much easier to control his depth than with the rebreather and there was no taste in the air he breathed.

On the bottom he began to find out other things about the lung. He liked the separate mask and breathing device for, with the rebreather, there was always the chance of something going wrong with the mask which covered your whole face and through which your air came. If something went wrong with the mask you could not only not see, but you couldn't breathe either. With the Aqua-Lung you breathed through a mouthpiece entirely separate from the mask, so even with no mask at all, you could keep on breathing until you got to the top again.

The plane was scattered all over the bottom, broken pieces of it everywhere. Ken swam slowly along, recognizing various parts—the tail section, a piece of the stabilizer, a ragged length of wing, the engine torn out of the nacelle.

Then he found one of the pilots. The man was lying on his back on the sand, his arms beside him, his legs bent a little. All blood had been washed away from the wound in his chest. He seemed to be lying there thirty feet below the surface sound asleep.

For a moment Ken looked at this dead man. This motionless thing lying at the bottom of the sea had, a few hours ago, tried to kill him.

Ken searched the dead Jap and found a small booklet covered with brown canvas in one of his pockets. Then, in the debris of the cockpit, he found a folded chart and two more canvas-covered booklets. He could find no evidence of radar anywhere even though nothing seemed to have been blown up.

The other pilot had been torn apart and was hardly recognizable as a man.

Knowing that the two pilots would soon draw sharks, Ken wrapped up what he had found and started for the surface, where he could see the yellow bottom of the rubber boat bounding around.

As he came up he decided that the rebreather had only one advantage over the Aqua-Lung. No bubbles came out of the rebreather, for all oxygen was contained in the system. With the Aqua-Lung bubbles streamed up with each breath.

Ken decided that in daytime work, where there was a possibility of being spotted by bubbles, he'd use the rebreather. Otherwise he was sold on the Aqua-Lung.

He got back to his cabin in the *Shark* as the ship's bell rang eight times.

Si Mount, sitting up in bed, said, "Eight bells. Let's get *out* of here."

Carney's voice sounded through the ship. "Start engines."

CHAPTER 11

THE PULSING OF THE DIESELS idly turning over felt good to Ken as he went through the control room and climbed on up into the conning tower. They seemed to bring life back into the *Shark;* to promise that soon they would be back in the open sea. Soon they would be free from this land and no longer just a target for anything the Japs might have around.

Ken climbed on up through the conning tower to the bridge, where Carney, Doherty, and Bill Adams were waiting.

"Post sea details," Carney said through the loud-speakers. "Stand by to get under way."

Then he grinned at Ken. "I hope that's not just some wishful thinking."

"She'll come off," Doherty declared, looking down at the water, now high around the sides of the boat. "If she doesn't we'll lighten ship."

Carney nodded. Then he frowned a little. "If we have to lighten, Frank, let's dump the fish last. Everything else goes over the side first."

"Aye, aye, Skipper."

"We'll get out of this bay on the surface, then get down under the water where we belong," Carney said. "All engines back full."

Ken looked astern. As the propellers began to turn over they threw up around the tumble home a great, boiling mass of sand and water. It swept forward and began to break like surf on the beach at the bow.

Carney called for more power and Ken felt the diesels

grow stronger, the dirty waves of water rising higher.

Bill Adams said, "She's beginning to move."

At their feet the Chief Electrician poked his head up out of the hatch. "The radar's fouled up again, Captain," he said. "The set's working OK but nothing's being fed into it."

"What do you think's wrong with it then?" Carney asked as the boat backed slowly away from the island.

"Did that airplane hit the antenna, Captain?"

Carney glanced up at the revolving antenna. "No sign of it, Chief, but it could have. It was close enough. We'll fix it when we surface tonight. Starboard engine stop. Port engine back."

The *Shark* began to swing around.

"Starboard engine ahead full."

The boat swung faster, its bow coming around toward the open mouth of the bay.

"Port engine stop. Starboard engine stop."

"Steady on the helm. Course two seven zero."

"Steady on two seven zero, sir."

"All ahead one half."

Bells rang down inside the boat as it started slowly forward, heading out of the bay.

Ken went down the ladder into the conning tower, where the sea detail was already on watch. The radarman was looking at the screen with a baffled expression. The soundman was just putting on his earphones as he flipped switches and began turning the big dial.

Ken dropped on down to control and went forward. In the cabin with Si, he said, "Under way again. Slid off nice as you please."

"Good," Si said. "I'm a nervous wreck. Boy, think of how the Marines must feel sitting on a beach the way we were."

Ken got the air cylinder he had used with the Aqua-Lung and started forward to look up the chief and see about getting it refilled.

He was just stepping down into the forward torpedo room when he heard the soundman say, "High-speed screws, Captain. Bearing two five nine. Distance ten thousand. Sounds like a can, Captain."

Suddenly, dropping down through the open hatch, a man almost fell on Ken. He had on nothing but ragged shorts. He yelled at the chief, "A Jap destroyer is coming into the bay!"

The chief yelled back, "*Shut that hatch!*"

Two men sprang to the hatch, shut it with a crash, and swung the bright steel dogging handles.

"You think the can saw us?" the chief asked.

"Couldn't help it," the bare-chested man said. "He's right on top of us."

Carney's voice sounded calm through the loudspeaker. "Dive the boat."

As the diving Klaxon began, the chief looked over at Ken. "We can't move inside this bay. All right, you guys, get on these tubes."

"What are we going to shoot at?" a man asked even as he jumped to the after end of a torpedo tube. "That can's coming straight at us."

Carney said through the loud-speaker, "A Jap destroyer has trapped us in the bay so we're coming out shootin'."

When Carney stopped they could still hear voices in the conning tower. A man near Ken said petulantly, "Somebody goofed and left the mike button open."

Another man, his face so white that his eyes seemed unnaturally bright and wet, turned to the chief. "We can't shoot at him that way, Chief. We'll miss him."

The chief, his face suddenly much older, just nodded.

Carney said, "Make ready forward tubes. Set depth eight feet."

Men leaped to dials on the sides of the tubes. The chief, standing perfectly still, watched them and then nodded to the man on the telephone. "Tubes ready forward. Depth set, eight feet."

"Match gyros forward," Carney said.

The chief turned and watched the man on the gyro compass. Then he nodded again to the talker.

"Stand by forward."

In the torpedo room not a man moved. Those who were not on the firing detail stayed clear, some sitting on the bunks, others standing against the bulkhead. Every man in the crowded room stared at the red lights glowing on each tube.

"Up periscope!"

"Continuous bearings."

In the torpedo room they could hear the bearing reader's singsong chant.

Then they heard Doherty say nervously, "Periscope's been up a long time, Skipper."

Carney said, "I want it up. I want him to see it and come straight at it. It's the only chance we've got, Frank."

One of the men near Ken said, "We can't hit him coming straight at us."

"What should we do then?" a young seaman asked.

"There's nothing we can do," the gunner said. "He'll either ram us or get on top of us and unload everything he's got."

The seaman's voice went up a notch. "What's wrong with the Skipper? Why doesn't he *do* something?"

The chief, looking old now and tired, walked slowly over to the seaman. "Take it easy, son. You'll live longer."

"I'm not going to live at all!" the seaman screamed at him. "The periscope's up. They can *see* us! What's the matter with the Skipper?"

The chief, his voice quiet and friendly, said, "What would you do if you were the Skipper?"

The seaman was still screaming. "I'd get that scope down and dodge. I'd get *away* from him!"

"Not inside a bay with only sixty feet of water, you wouldn't," the chief said.

A man sitting on a bunk said bitterly, "This boat hasn't had a real skipper since they launched her. Now we're going to get the works."

The chief turned around. Ken was startled by the change in his expression. He no longer looked old and tired. Nor did he look angry as he said, "Pipe down. This boat's got a skipper now. Do you think it's easy for Mr. Carney to look through that periscope and see nothing but the bow of a Jap can coming down on him? Do you think you could do it and keep on thinking and paying attention? No, you couldn't. You'd take one look at that bow slicing through the water and you'd yell for Mama. Now you remember this: this boat's got *plenty* of skipper."

Then Carney said, "Attention in the boat. This is Carney. A Japanese destroyer is bearing down straight at us dead ahead. There isn't enough water to go under him. There isn't enough room to get around him. He intends to ram, I think. We just have time for one salvo but, coming straight at us this way makes him a very small and hard-to-hit target. If we miss him he will ram. All hands stand by to abandon ship through the escape hatches. Break out all Momsen lungs. And remember, if you're taken prisoner tell them nothing except your name, your rate, and your serial number. That's all. Good luck."

From conn Ken could hear the soundman chanting, "Two thousand five. Two thousand four. Two thousand three."

The chief said, "That boy's barreling in here."

The seaman cried, "Why don't we shoot? What's the matter?"

The chief looked over at him. "Son, when we shoot it's going to be so close that that can won't be able to turn an inch to dodge 'em. That's when we're going to shoot if Mr. Carney does things the way I think he will."

The bearing reader: "Zero on the bow. Zero. Zero."

Carney sounded perfectly calm. "Get her absolutely steady on the helm."

"Helm steady, sir."

The telephone talker went past Ken, trailing his phone line, and stood beside the chief. "The Skipper wants to know if you're all set, Chief?"

"Tell him we're set."

"The Skipper says this is going to be a kill-or-miss shot, Chief."

"Tell him I know that," the chief said.

"The Skipper says good luck, Chief."

"Tell him that if we come out of this one *I'll* buy *him* a steak dinner at P. Y. Chong's."

"He says it's a deal, Chief."

The soundman: "One thousand five. One thousand four. One thousand three."

Ken's hands were sweating.

A first class petty officer said, "If we hit with a shot like this they'll never believe it in Pearl."

"We'll never see Pearl again," the seaman said. "We'll never get out of this bay again."

Then Willy came in. He had a small metal tray with a pile of sandwiches covered with a clean, damp, white cloth. "You hungry, Mr. Braden?"

"Not right now, Willy. Thanks."

Willy looked disappointed. "You hungry, Chief?"

"*No*, Willy. Thanks."

"Well," Willy said, sitting down on a bunk, "no use wasting all these good sandwiches." He began to eat as he, too, stared at the red lights on the torpedo tubes. "Book says you can't do this," Willy declared.

"Do what?" Ken asked.

"Book says never shoot at anybody's bow. Book says you bound to miss and then, since he's coming your way anyway, he's going to swarm all over you. That's what the book says."

The chief picked up one of the sandwiches, then put it down again. "It's a good thing our Skipper never read the book."

The soundman: "One thousand. Nine hundred five. Nine hundred."

The chief turned back to face the tubes.

Doherty, in conn, said, "Set. Set. Set."

"If any of you guys want to pray," the chief said, "do it now."

None of the men moved but it seemed to Ken that on each man's face there was a change, a deepening of expression.

"FIRE!"

The deck of the boat slid under Ken's feet.

"FIRE!"

It slid again.

The telephone talker said, "Number one fired electrically. Number two fired electrically."

"FIRE!"

"Number three fired electrically."

"FIRE!"

There were strange sounds in the tubes—as though some monstrous animal were gulping in water. First there was the backward pouring of water into the tubes and then the hiss of air as the boat drank the air in rather than have it bubble out the end of the tube.

"Go, little gals," the chief said. "Go, little gals." Then he turned to Ken. "Now we wait."

"What's the run time, Chief?" a man asked.

"I'd give number one ten on the outside. Eight for two."

Down through the water and through the double steel hulls of the boat and into the room with them came the *thum thum thum* of the Jap destroyer's propellers. *Thum thum thum.*

The soundman: "All torpedoes running hot and straight."

Someone in the conning tower was counting seconds.

Carney ordered, "Stand by five and six."

The chief said, "Tell him we're ready."

The time counter droned on: ". . . three seconds . . . two seconds . . . one second . . . zero. Number one should be there, Skipper."

Thum thum thum

Carney: "Down periscope."

Thum thum thum

Soundman: "Number one still running hot and true, but fading."

"We missed," the chief said.

Thum thum thum

". . . two seconds . . . one second . . . zero."

THUM THUM THUM

Soundman: "Number two fading, sir."

THUM THUM THUM

Soundman: "Four hundred. . . ."

"We missed," the chief said.

THUM THUM THUM

WHANG

There was sudden thunder and lightning in the boat. The deck disappeared under Ken's feet and he felt himself floating.

Carney's voice sounded far away—in another world—as he said, "Hard left rudder. All ahead full."

W H A N G

As Ken fell against a bunk the ship heaved again and he was thrown all the way across the room.

Carney: "Come around to two seven zero. Sound, what do you hear?"

Soundman: "He's too close to make it out, sir. But his screws have stopped."

"Is he on top of us?"

"No, sir. Just abeam now. About a hundred feet away."

"Up periscope."

Ken picked himself up off the deck as the whine of the periscope motors sounded through the boat.

Now, outside, he could hear strange sounds. Metal was straining and breaking, there were hissings and bubblings and grindings, and there were many little explosions and tinkling sounds.

Carney said, "He's going . . . going. . . . He's down with all hands. Down periscope. Sound, keep the depth coming."

Soundman: "Seventy five . . . eighty . . . ninety . . . one hundred. . . ."

Carney: "Take her down to sixty feet. Frank, are those patches on number two still holding?"

"Tight as a drum, Skipper."

"Depth sixty feet."

In the torpedo room men began to move and talk again. Color began to come back into their faces.

The talker said, "The Skipper says nice shooting, Chief."

The chief only nodded.

"The Skipper says you owe him a steak dinner at P. Y. Chong's, Chief."

The chief looked for a long time at the slick steel floor. Then he raised his head. "Tell the Skipper that's one I don't mind losing. No, not at all, I don't."

The first class petty officer said, almost whispering, "He rammed it right down his throat. Right down his throat. They won't believe it when I tell 'em in Pearl. It can't be done."

The seaman, his face a blank, said, "We hit him. We hit him, didn't we?"

The chief turned and looked at him. "Sure we hit him. What'd you expect, son? We got a *Skipper* on this boat."

140

Willy said, "Look like somebody ought to want a sandwich. I go to all that trouble making 'em and nobody'll eat 'em."

The chief took a sandwich and bit into it. "What you got in here, Willy? Battery plates?"

"Couldn't get any battery plates, Chief. Sparks said he couldn't spare me any."

Ken, too, took a sandwich. Then he noticed the air cylinder he had put down on one of the bunks.

Suddenly it seemed to him that a thousand years had passed since he had come into the torpedo room to see the chief about refilling the air cylinder.

A thousand years.

PART III—MIDNIGHT

CHAPTER 1

ALL DAY LONG THE *Shark* had been moving, submerged, toward the atoll. Now the air in the boat was flat and stale and contained a thousand odors. It smelled and tasted of diesel fuel and hot oil; there was the peculiar odor of ozone from the brushes on the motor commutators; there was the smell of rubber, linoleum, old and fresh sweat; the faintly acrid odor from the heads; of cooking. When you breathed it felt as if you had not drawn in enough air; that it didn't do you much good.

It was hot in the boat, too. An oppressive, still heat which fans and blowers seemed only to move from one place to another. This moving heat struck you and flowed around you and didn't cool you.

As the long day wore on, men looked more and more at the clocks on the bulkheads, or their watches, waiting for nightfall. Then the boat would go back to the surface. The hatches would be opened and the powerful blowers would drive the cool, sweet, fresh, ocean air down into the boat, forcing it into each compartment and space and forcing out this stuff which left a taste on your tongue with every breath you took.

Ken finished his day's study of the Japanese language and, taking his books and papers, went across to the cabin he shared with Si Mount and Pat Malone.

Si, his wounded leg propped up on pillows, looked tired and drawn when Ken came in. "How long before we get some decent air?"

"Couple of hours."

"You can cut this stuff with a knife."

Ken nodded as he put away his books. "Want that bandage changed?"

Si looked up at him. "I sure do."

Ken cut the old bandage off and looked at the wound in Si's leg. It had healed nicely, leaving only two purplish-red areas where the bullet had gone in and come out. As he put on fresh bandages, Si said, "I'm going to get up."

"It'll be all right if you take it easy."

"I'd love to get over to the wardroom. Just to sit around a little while."

"Long enough to get the sheets changed on this sack, anyway," Ken told him. "The place smells like a fox den."

"I've been thinking about Phil Carney," Si said as Ken kept on wrapping the bandages. "That must have been hard—watching the destroyer coming down on us. It's bad enough to make an attack on a destroyer when he doesn't know where you are. A can is hard to hit even with a perfect shot on his beam, and if you miss him it's just—Katie bar the door. But to do it the way Phil did ... He knew that if he missed we were gone. But it was the only chance he had and he took it. I wonder what Stevenson would have done?"

"I don't know," Ken admitted. "Maybe the same thing."

"He might have," Si agreed. "But I wonder if he would have been steady enough for it. The way Phil did it was a beautiful piece of timing. He had to give the fish enough distance to arm themselves and settle down after being fired. But, at the same time, he didn't give the can enough distance to escape them after they were

143

sighted. They must have seen 'em coming, but the way Phil set it up there was nowhere the can could go without getting one. Nice."

Ken got some clean clothes for Si and helped him put them on.

"By the way," Si said, "has Phil said anything about how he's going to get you ashore on the islands?"

"Not a word."

"Has he got the op plan you made for Stevenson?"

He nodded.

Si frowned. "That's funny. If he's not going to do it the way Stevenson planned it, looks like he'd have said something to you about it, doesn't it?"

"He may not have had time."

"He's had plenty of time."

"Maybe tonight. Nobody can think in air this foul."

"Has he moved into the Skipper's cabin?"

Ken nodded. "Willy moved him this morning. You all set?" He helped Si get to his feet. "How does it feel?"

"Weak and wobbly, but it doesn't hurt much." Si looked at himself in the mirror. "Oh, horrid!" he said, rubbing the tangled beard he had grown. "I look worse than Malone. I never knew a skeleton could grow a beard."

By holding on to the doorjamb, Si pulled himself out into the corridor. Then, leaning on Ken, he walked over to the wardroom and sat down, stretching his leg out as far as he could.

Willy stuck his head through the little opening from the service pantry. "Hi, Mr. Si," he said. "You navigating again?"

"Just dead reckoning, Willy."

"You want some java and a sandwich?"

"Just some java, Willy."

"You ought to eat something," Willy told him. "You look thin as a pin. How about a bacon and egg sandwich? I got some good eggs—not more'n a month old.

You hold your nose and don't look and they go down real easy."

"OK, Willy."

"I'll toast that sandwich and spread some of this air on it so you won't notice the egg so much."

When Willy went out Ken asked, "Does he ever sleep?"

Si laughed. "Pat says he caught him asleep one time sitting on a stool, but he's the only one."

Before Willy got back Carney said over the loud-speaker, "Prepare to surface."

"Good," Si said. "I always get a headache at the end of a day's run under the water."

"Surface!" The Klaxon sounded harshly and Ken felt the angle of the deck change. Soon they could hear the superstructure breaking the surface of the water, the sea piling down the sides of the bridge, then pouring off the decks.

The main induction opened with a crash, and at the order to start engines, the diesels began to throb.

"Don't see how," Si said, "but they seem to get this boat up and down without my advice."

The first blast of fresh air felt almost cold as it came rushing down into the wardroom. Si leaned back and breathed deeply. "This is a time in the submarines I always like," he said. "That first breath of real air when you come up at night. You look forward to it all day long."

Now the boat was rolling a little and pitching in the sea as it moved through the surface waves. Under water there was no movement except straight ahead—not even a feeling of movement—although you could hear the electric motors running and the swish of the propellers.

Willy came back with sandwiches and coffee. "Dog if they didn't blow all that air out of the boat before I could spread you some."

As Si started to eat, Carney poked his head into the wardroom. "How you feeling, Si?"

145

"Better, sir. You can put me back on the watch list."

"No hurry. Ken's turned into a good communicator."

"That was a nice shot, Skipper," Si said.

Carney seemed to think about it for a moment, then said, "Pat and Frank set that one up."

"Who was on the periscope with you?" Si asked.

"Pat was my dancing partner. Frank had the target data computer. We missed you on the firing setup."

"It was nice," Si said again.

"Nice setup. He turned hard to starboard to miss the first one and the second one missed too, but that third one got him right where he lived. Ken, if you're not too busy, how about getting off that dispatch to Pearl. Have you still got it?"

"Yes, sir. The one about Commander Stevenson?"

"That's it. Let me know what COMSUBPAC says, will you? I'll be in my cabin—I mean, the Skipper's cabin. Take it easy, Si. We've got a couple of days to go and you might as well sack out until we get to the atoll."

Si nodded as Carney went out.

"You want me to help you back before I go?" Ken asked.

"Let me stay here. Somebody might come in and want to play a little acey-deucy."

"You feel all right?"

"Fine. It's a relief to be out of that bed."

Ken got the dispatch and went down to the radio shack. The first class, Shelton, had the watch.

Ken encoded the dispatch about Stevenson's death and handed it to Shelton, who sent it and then sat back in his chair. "It's after midnight in Pearl so they'll have to wake somebody up to get any action on that. Probably be an hour or so."

"I'll wait," Ken said, sitting down on the wastebasket.

Shelton put on one earphone and lit a cigarette. "Java?"

"Just had some. You want some?"

"No, thanks. Just finished chow." Shelton glanced at the clock on the bulkhead. "FOX'll be coming in in a minute or two."

Ken vaguely remembered that FOX was a channel on which messages to the entire Navy were sent.

"Here she comes," Shelton said, putting on the other phone.

He listened intently for some minutes and then said, "Nothing for us."

Ken could hear the code snapping in the earphones. It sounded incredibly fast and he wondered how anyone could read it.

"Whoa, whoa," Shelton said, grabbing a pencil and beginning to write. "Sounds like a promotion ALNAV."

Ken wasn't sure, but he thought an ALNAV was a message for all the Navy.

Shelton stopped writing and went on listening.

Ken watched the clock hand slide past eleven-thirty as he waited.

The FOX broadcast ended and Shelton shoved back one of the earphones. Then he rummaged through the desk drawers until he found the ship's roster. "What do you know," he said, running his finger down the signal numbers. "That ALNAV caught Mr. Malone. See? All ensigns between 150,000 and 160,000 get promoted and he's 155,165. That's good. He deserves it." Shelton handed him the piece of paper. "Will you give it to him?"

As Ken nodded, Shelton shoved the other phone back on. "Pearl's calling us." He began to write, and in a few moments, handed Ken the piece of paper with the groups of letters on it.

He put the strips in the coding board and went to work.

By the time he finished it was midnight and the Boatswain's Mate was calling to relieve the watch.

He thanked Shelton and went back to the Skipper's cabin.

Carney was studying some papers when he came into the tiny cabin. "Sit down, Ken," Carney said, waving toward the bed. He put the papers away as Ken handed him the dispatch, which read:

LIEUTENANT CARNEY ASSUME TEMPORARY COMMAND OF SHARK STOP LIEUTENANT DOHERTY APPOINTED TEMPORARY EXECUTIVE OFFICER STOP PROCEED ON MISSION STOP COMSUB-PAC SENDS.

Carney nodded his head and put the dispatch in the folder. "That was what I've been waiting for. Can you spare a minute, Ken?"

"Yes, sir."

"Not sleepy?"

"No, sir."

"We're going ahead with the mission. I've just been going over that op plan you made. Did you and Paul agree on it?"

Ken suddenly remembered the way the word mutiny looked in the dictionary. "Sir, I don't know exactly how to say this and I guess it isn't the Navy way, but just before Commander Stevenson got killed, I was on my way to tell him that I wasn't going to risk my life trying to do things according to that op plan. Maybe that's mutiny, I don't know."

He stopped and looked straight at Carney. Then he went on. "I'm still not going to do it, sir."

"I don't blame you," Carney said. "That isn't mutiny. That's suicide the way it's planned. Useless suicide at that."

Ken kept looking straight at him. "Are you going into the lagoon, Captain?"

Carney nodded. "It's the only way. I don't like it; it's dangerous, but it's the only way I can see to do it."

"Me, too," Ken said.

148

Carney handed him the sheaf of papers. "Will you work up another op plan? Base it on our entering the lagoon at twenty-one hundred and leaving at oh four hundred. That gives you seven hours."

"That ought to be enough, Skipper."

"When you get it roughed out, let's get together on it, Ken."

"Aye, aye, sir. And—thanks."

Carney glanced over at him and then smiled. "For what, Ken? For taking you into the middle of a hornets' nest?"

"No," Ken said. "For taking the boat into the lagoon, where, if I get off the island, I can find it when I come back."

On the way across to the wardroom he paused. There was still an odor in the air in the boat, still a tinge of staleness. He decided that he could think a lot better if he went topside and breathed some really pure air for a little while.

He stuck his head in the wardroom and asked Si who had the deck. Si looked at the watch list and told him Pat was up there.

When Ken got into the control room, where there were open hatches leading up to the bridge, he could hear Malone's voice singing:

> *"Oh, a capital ship for an ocean trip*
> *Was the Walloping Window-blind. . . ."*

Ken climbed up into the conning tower.

> *"No gale that blew dismayed her crew*
> *Or troubled the Captain's mind. . . ."*

In the dim light Ken took off one of the silver lieutenant (j.g.) bars on his shirt collar.

Malone's voice was louder, clearer:

> *"The man at the wheel was taught to feel*
> *Contempt for the wildest blow. . . ."*

Ken climbed up to the darkness of the bridge. Malone was leaning against the splinter shield singing into the wind as a working party of electricians made shadowy figures around the radar antenna.

Malone bellowed:

> *"And it often appeared when the weather had cleared,*
> *That he'd been in his bunk beee—low."*

Malone saw him and said, "Hiya, ol' pardner, ol' pardner. Or did you know that I'm an ol' slowpoke from Texas?"

"No, I didn't."

"I'm not. Help yourself to some air, courtesy of the Emperor of Japan, no less."

"Tastes good," Ken said. "Here." He held out his hand.

"Ha," Malone said, taking the silver bar. "And what might this be now?" He took it over to the dim red chart light and looked at it. "Did somebody lose this badge of authority, this insignia of the mighty class of lieutenants junior grade?"

"No," Ken said, "it's yours."

"Well now, and begosh and begorra, I 'ave no need for the filthy thing. I, sir, am an ensign."

"You *were* an ensign." He unfolded the ALNAV under the light.

Malone studied it for a long time, turning the lieutenant's bar over and over between his fingers. "You didn't make this up, did you, Ken?"

"Nope. I heard it come in on the FOX."

"Truly?"

"On my word."

Malone looked at the silver bar. "Well, I'll be damned." Then, in silence, he took the two gold bars of an ensign off his ragged shirt collar. He looked at them lying in his hand then flipped them into the sea.

"Lookout," he called.

"Lookout, aye, aye."

"From now on let's have a little respect around here," Malone told him. "I want you to know that I am, at last, a lieutenant."

"That right?" the lookout asked.

"That is right."

"Congratulations, Mr. Malone. You really rate it."

"Thanks, boy, thanks." Pat then turned to Ken. "Feels good, doesn't it? *Real* good. I've waited a long time."

CHAPTER 2

"ALL AHEAD SLOW," CARNEY SAID. Then he added, "Just keep steerageway on her, Bill. And stand by for all back emergency."

Then he turned to the man on the helm. "If we touch anything going through here we're going to back and then spin her right around."

"Aye, aye, sir."

"Up periscope."

The periscope motors whined somewhere below and the shiny, oily shaft slid up through the deck of the conning tower. Carney unfolded the handles and stooped to the eyepiece. He swung the scope from side to side. "Down periscope. We're in the entrance now. The lagoon is dead ahead and there's land on each side of us. If the Japs have got this lagoon closed off with a net we should be finding it out any minute now. Up periscope."

The soundman chanted, "Depth six zero zero . . . six zero zero . . . six one zero . . . six two zero. . . ."

"Down periscope. At least we've got plenty of water under us," Carney said. "Dead slow, Bill."

"Dead slow, Skipper."

"Heads up on the bow and stern planes. If we have to spin her, let's keep her under the water."

At such slow speed there was little noise in the sub.

"Up periscope. We're in the lagoon now. There's no moon, but a skyful of stars. Down periscope. Ask Lieutenant Braden if he's all set."

In a moment the talker said, "Lieutenant Braden reports all set."

"Tell him we're feeling our way into the lagoon now. He's got about twenty minutes. Up periscope."

He left the scope up for about ten seconds. "I can see lights on Midnight Island. Two sets of them. The ones on the northern end are brighter than the one in the center of the island. Report that to Lieutenant Braden, please. Down periscope."

Ken, standing below the inboard end of the escape hatch, listened as the talker reported the lights Carney could see. "Wonder what he sees on the other islands," he said to Pat Malone.

As though in answer they heard the periscope motor whine, and in a moment, the talker said, "The captain says he doesn't see light on any of the other islands."

Ken nodded. "I'll hit Midnight first."

Pat looked at his watch. "Three minutes to twelve. You've got about fifteen minutes."

Ken had on a shirt over the gray swimming suit. He peeled it off and picked up the harness of the Aqua-Lung. Pat held the cylinder up for him as he got the straps over his shoulders and up between his legs. When he had the cross strap in place on his chest he closed the quick-release buckle and reached back for the two hoses which ended in the rubber mouthpiece. Next he put the face mask on, but left it pushed back up on his forehead. "I'll put the fins on after I get in there."

"The captain says no sign of boats in the water," the talker said.

Pat picked up a clip-board with Ken's check-off list. "'Lung'?" he read.

Ken put the mouthpiece in, clamping his teeth down on the two little nipples and then shoving the thin rubber flanges up under his lips. Opening the valve of the air tank, he breathed two or three times, then closed the valve and spat out the mouthpiece. "Lung, OK."

"'Mask'?" Pat read.

"Mask, OK."

" 'Watch'?"

Ken glanced at the wrist watch in the watertight case on his arm. It was now two minutes past midnight. "Watch, OK."

" 'Compass'?"

On his other wrist was a compass with bright radium on the dial and needle. "Compass, OK."

" 'Fins'?"

He picked them up. "Fins, OK."

" 'Dog tag'?"

He flicked the little aluminum plate with his name, serial number, and blood type stamped on it. "OK."

" 'Knife'?"

The knife was in a sheath on the weight belt.

Pat turned to the talker. "Ask for a time check, please."

In a moment they could hear a voice saying, "Stand by for zero zero zero seven. Thirty seconds . . . twenty . . . ten . . . five . . . four . . . three . . . two . . . one . . . Mark."

His watch was only a second or so off so he left it alone. "Time, OK."

"Time of return not later than oh four hundred."

"Oh four hundred."

Pat put the clip-board down. "That's it."

Ken nodded. He was covered with sweat. It was running down the middle of his chest and around the dog tag, and running down the backs of his legs. "Hot in here."

Pat glanced at him and said, "Yeah, sure is."

Ken felt a little sick in his stomach. There was a lot of cold spit running around his back teeth and it seemed hard to breathe. Also, he was beginning to tremble. First his hands began to shake and then his legs.

"Five minutes," Pat said.

Ken looked at him. Pat's face, the beard huge and black, was indistinct. It seemed to fade away and then swim back again. "I'm afraid I'm going to be sick," he said, not opening his teeth.

Pat pulled a bucket out of a bracket on the bulkhead and put it down on the deck. "Go ahead. It'll do you good."

Ken swallowed hard and held his lips pressed together. He caught one hand with the other and tried to make them stop shaking. At last, he said, "I'm scared."

"Who wouldn't be?" Pat asked cheerfully.

"I'm so scared I can't move."

He stood there, sick and shaking, and for the first time thought of fear. Up until right now he had never even considered it. But now, so weak with fear that he could barely stand up, so sick with it that he was on the verge of vomiting, he thought about it.

Right from the time he had held up his hand to volunteer for a "job" back at the UDT school; from the time he had sat in the admiral's office listening to the myna birds; from the time he and the admiral and Paul Stevenson had talked about Midnight Island—all along he had never once thought that, perhaps, he would be too afraid to do what they wanted him to do. He had never thought that his own fear would suddenly become a greater enemy to him than Stevenson's plans, the Japanese, the sea.

Suddenly he went down on his knees and vomited into the bucket. So weak now that he could not even stay upright on his knees, he almost fell before Pat caught him, holding his body up with one hand, his head with the other.

"Shoot the works, boy," Pat said.

Drained at last and empty, Ken sat weakly down on the deck. "That's the works."

Pat shoved the bucket away with his foot. Then he helped Ken back to his feet and over to the scuttlebutt. The water tasted clean and cool to Ken's raw throat.

He remembered now how afraid he had been during

the attack which had killed Paul Stevenson. Remembered now the way he had had to hold on to the splinter screen to keep from falling down when the plane was coming in on them back at Eugalin. Remembered swimming in fear in the forward torpedo room waiting for Carney's order to fire at the destroyer.

He knew now that he was too scared to go ashore on Midnight Island. There were Japanese there. Carney had let him look through the periscope that afternoon. At one end of the island there were several wood and concrete buildings and a radio mast. In the center there were about twenty of the native houses made of leaves and grass. He had seen, through the periscope, men in the dull, drab uniform of the Japanese Army walking between the buildings.

Pat went over to the escape hatch and opened the heavy, small, round door. "Time to go."

Ken nodded and, picking up the fins, walked over.

"You'll be all right," Pat said.

Ken said nothing as he climbed up into the escape hatch.

Before Pat closed the door he looked up into the tiny space. "OK?"

Ken nodded.

"When you're ready, hammer on the wall."

He nodded.

"Good luck, boy," Pat said. "See you around four in the morning."

Ken could only nod again.

The light in the escape hatch began rapidly to fade. Ken, not breathing at all, watched the steel door swing shut, the light fading and dying. Then, suddenly, there was no light at all.

He had never experienced such absolute darkness. It was so black in there that it was like a solid.

He stood still, listening to the sounds coming from

the submarine—the faint sounds of motors and fans, of people moving and talking, of metal striking metal.

He did not move. The rubber mouthpiece of the Aqua-Lung lay dangling on his chest from the two hoses. The face mask pressed against his forehead, the fins hung in his hands.

Suddenly light appeared again, the door swinging open. "You OK?" Pat asked.

Ken nodded.

"The Skipper says it's time to go, Ken."

"All right."

Then it was dark again.

He *had* to go. He couldn't face Carney and Si and Pat if he didn't go.

Then he thought of something. Even as it took shape he felt shame, like hot glue, on his skin.

He would go out of the escape hatch, swim up to the surface. Then he would just lie there in the water and let time pass. At four in the morning he would swim back down again and tell them . . . Tell them what? he wondered.

He would have plenty of time to make up a lie while he was lying in the water waiting for the time to pass.

He stooped and put the fins on his feet. Then he pulled the face mask down and made sure it was airtight by breathing in through his nose. He got the mouthpiece in and opened the valve, breathing now from the tank on his back.

With the butt end of the knife he hammered against the steel wall of the escape hatch.

Somewhere above him in the pitch blackness he heard something creak and then an avalanche of water crashed down on him. He felt it rising solidly up his body and then close over his head.

He floated straight up, feeling his way along with his hands. He didn't know when he finally left the *Shark* for, at sixty feet down, none of the starlight penetrated.

157

But, gradually as he went up, the water became less dark until, when he broke the surface, the night seemed bright.

Pushing the mask back, he looked up at the sky. He had never in his life seen so many stars. They were stuck to black velvet and shone with a flickering, cold, white light.

The water was calm and he could feel no wind at all. Spitting out the mouthpiece, he turned and looked toward the island.

The lights on Midnight seemed close. The ones on the Japanese end were bright and evidently electric, while the light in the center of the island was a soft, low, yellow which brightened and faded as a fire would.

The vomiting had taken away the sick feeling in his stomach and in the water he could no longer feel his hands and legs shaking.

In fact, he felt rather good. Free. Until now he had not realized how cramped it was in the submarine. You walked always with your shoulders hunched down and your head lowered to keep from knocking your brains out on the overhead piping. Now, in the water, he could stretch out—he had all the room in the world.

It was twenty minutes past twelve.

Slowly he began swimming toward the island. He could still feel his shame like something stuck to him as he swam along awkwardly with the big tank strapped to his back.

The southern end of the island showed no light at all. Turning that way, he could soon hear the sea washing on the beach stirring the sand and broken shells.

He went carefully now, just swimming with his hands until he touched bottom.

Lying there with only his head above water, he searched the dark trees and the long, curving beach. To the south the sand stretched on and on until it ended in the sea. To the north he could see no houses, nor, from so low, could he see the yellow glow of firelight. He could, however, still see in the sky the reflected glow from the Japanese lights.

Moving slowly, he crawled out of the water. Then, only an inch or two at a time, he moved across the beach.

The darkness under the trees felt good to him. Pulling the quick-release buckle, he let the Aqua-Lung down to the sand and stepped out of the fins.

With one fin he dug a hole near the base of a palm and buried the lung, the fins, mask, and belt. Then he covered and concealed the hole.

When he was through he stood up and looked toward the glow in the sky from the Japanese lights.

Now he had on only the wrist watch, the gray swimming suit which covered him from neck to ankles, and his dog tag.

At least, he thought, it won't be a lie when I tell them that I got ashore.

He began sneaking along through the shadows.

He would, he thought, just look around a little. He wouldn't, he decided, get into any danger.

CHAPTER 3

A LOW, SMOKELESS FIRE WAS BURNING on the hard-packed ground. The flame's yellow glow was like liquid gold falling first on a circle of dark-skinned people and then, fading, falling on the houses built in a row along a wide cleared space.

Ken had hidden himself behind a palm tree out of range of the light and close enough to the beach for him to be able to see anyone approaching him from behind.

For a long time he studied the scene around the fire. Each of the natives was sitting on a mat woven out of the fronds of the palms. They sat almost motionless and rarely spoke. When they did it was in voices so low that he could not make out even the language they used.

Occasionally a woman would get up and go into one of the houses. Sometimes she would come back, sometimes she would not.

The men were dressed only in loincloths. Ken could see that these were made of ragged bits of cloth, much patched. A few of the women also wore short skirts of cloth but most of them wore only skirts which Ken finally figured out must have been made from the flimsy, cloth-like bark of the coconut palm.

In the firelight their skins looked dark gold, their hair was long, straight, and black.

Except for some of the women, they were all old people. There was not, he noticed, a single young man in the group—only old men, hunched and wrinkled.

They sat on and on, doing nothing, saying very little. Some of them nodded as though sleepy; occasionally a woman would get up and put more wood on the fire.

It seemed to Ken as he watched them that they were waiting. For what, he couldn't tell. But they were waiting.

It was now fifteen minutes to one. Why, he wondered, were these people sitting here this late at night—just sitting and nodding before the fire?

He was, he knew, in little or no danger from these women and old men. Danger lay ahead of him; lay below the glow of light on the Japanese end.

He could go no farther without—at each step—increasing the danger.

He had to make a decision—now.

It was so simple. He could turn now and sneak away to tell a lie. Or—he could go ahead, risking his life by doing it.

Which way to go? If he went north his life might come to an end tonight. If he went south he would live tonight and for years to come—live with this shame now on him like some nastiness.

Ken, moving so slowly that he seemed not to move at all, left the place with its almost silent people.

His shame—as though it were a cloak—dropped from his shoulders and he left it lying there on Midnight Island.

He almost went past the tiny clearing without noticing it—only a murmur in the darkness caught his attention.

There, lit only by starlight, was another group of natives. These were huddled close together in the darkness.

They were all young men.

Close to them was a palm with two broken, hanging fronds, wide ones, and coming almost to the ground.

Watching the men always, Ken moved from shadow to shadow until he reached the fronds. Then he waited until a little breath of wind blew across the island and rustled the living fronds softly and dryly rattled the dead ones.

While the sound made by the wind lasted, Ken slipped inside the shelter of the leaves.

Through a slit in the dead stuff he could now clearly see the group of men.

Their talk was as low as that of the other group but Ken, being so much closer, could hear the words and phrases distinctly. It was not a language that he knew.

And then, quite clearly, one of the men said, "Speak in English so that they will not understand."

In the starlight Ken saw a glint of metal. One of the men had an old-fashioned watch tied by a string around his neck. The glint he had seen had come from the case as the man opened the watch and held it face up to the sky. "It is time," he said.

A man turned toward the Japanese end of the island and whistled. It was a low, sweet, soft sound—like the low song of night birds Ken had heard on Eugalin.

From the Japanese end of the island the whistle was returned—once, twice—five times.

Ken, hidden in the darkness, his back against the warm, rough trunk of the tree, wondered what this was all about. The answering whistles had come from five different distances and, from the varying strength of them, made him think that the men who had answered were posted at intervals all the way across the island.

Were they sentries? Lookouts? If they were, then what were they looking for? What were they guarding?

A man in the group got up and walked to the base of a tree. Ken could not see clearly what he was doing as he knelt down, his back to him.

Soon the man came back carrying a grayish box in his arms. He put this carefully down and then knelt beside it.

Ken waited for him to open the box, but he did not, nor did he move as he knelt there.

Suddenly, low, but distinct, Ken heard a high-pitched whine which descended smoothly and then stopped.

162

As he was trying to place the whine in his memory—it was a sound he had heard before—a woman's voice, cheerful and intimate, said, "Radio Tokyo calling. Radio Tokyo now presents the American hour. I have some new records tonight, but before I play them for you, I want to tell you foolish Americans what is happening to you. . . ."

The men had drawn close around the radio set and were absolutely silent as the woman's voice went cheerfully on.

"Oh, you Americans are so *stupid*. Didn't you learn any lessons from your terrible defeat at Pearl Harbor? Why do you keep sending your ships and planes into the Pacific? The Imperial Japanese Navy is simply waiting to sink or shoot them down and to drown you foolish sailors. And, today, you have committed the greatest folly of all. You have stupidly attacked one of our great fortresses. You have sent your poor marines against our island of Tarawa. This morning the warmongers who rule America forced thousands of poor, innocent American boys to try to reach the beaches of Tarawa. Now, tonight, they lie dead in the sea, their bodies being devoured by crabs and fishes—thousands and thousands of young boys. Listen to me, you sailors and marines of America, don't let those bloodthirsty old men in Washington do this to you. Don't let them murder you. I will now play an appropriate record."

From the radio, softly, came the pretty music of Guy Lombardo playing "What Is This Thing Called Love?"

It was six minutes to one.

When the record ended the woman began again. "At Tarawa we have already sunk seven destroyers, three cruisers, and the aircraft carrier *Liscombe Bay*, which went down with one thousand men. On the beaches more than eight thousand Americans are dead and the rest are being pushed relentlessly back into the sea, where they must drown, for there is no longer an American fleet afloat to pick them up."

She played another record.

It was two minutes to one.

The woman began to speak again. "And here is a warning to all American submarines. Stay home. Stay out of the Pacific. Units of the Imperial Japanese Navy are sinking your submarines whenever they are foolish enough to come beyond the Hawaiian Islands. We have just sunk two American submarines. One of these was the *Wahoo*, commanded by Dudley Morton. This foolish Mr. Morton had the audacity to bring his submarine with its crew of unfortunate men into the Sea of Japan. Of course they are all dead now. The other was the *Shark*, commanded by Paul Stevenson. The *Shark* was sunk with all hands by our gallant aviators. This is Radio Tokyo signing off the American hour."

It was one o'clock.

The regenerative whine from the radio sounded again as the kneeling man tuned it. He missed the station identification but the voice now announcing was unmistakably American.

"This is a communiqué from the Headquarters of the Commander-in-Chief, Pacific Ocean Areas.

"Today, forces of the United States Navy, Marine Corps, and Army attacked the Japanese-held Gilbert Islands in the Central Pacific area. Units of the Army made a successful landing on Makin Island and found almost no opposition there, the Japanese force being estimated at around five hundred men.

"Units of the United States Marine Corps are attacking the islands of Tarawa, which are the central bastion of Japanese strength in this area and are heavily fortified. The Japanese force defending the islands is estimated to be about ten thousand men.

"Since H-hour at oh nine hundred this morning we have gained a foothold on the islands in spite of extremely high casualties. However, the issue of the battle is still in doubt."

The kneeling man turned the radio off, picked it up, and went back to the tree with it. When he returned to the group one of them gave a low, birdlike whistle. Again it was answered five times.

In a little while Ken saw two men approaching from the Japanese end of the island. Then, one by one, three more. The five joined the group and Ken heard one ask, "What was the news?"

"Bad," a man answered. "The Americans have attacked the Gilbert Islands. Tokyo says that they have been repelled with heavy losses. The Americans admitted many casualties and that the battle has not been decided."

"How can they win if the Japanese sink all their ships?"

"The Americans are never coming," a man said quietly, his voice full of despair. "We will starve to death here under the Japanese before the Americans will come. Every man and woman and child will be destroyed by the Japanese."

"Wait," a man said. "The Americans haven't been defeated at Tarawa yet. They might win. We will listen again tomorrow night."

The man who had operated the radio shook his head. "We mustn't listen again so soon. The battery is almost finished."

"Why listen at all?" the first man asked. "The Americans will never come."

Ken hesitated only a second. There was no doubt in his mind about whose side these natives were on. If they would help him it would make his whole job easier.

He pushed the fronds gently aside and stepped toward the group. In a low voice he said, "I am an American and I am here."

He was surprised at the reaction of the men. For a

165

long moment not one of them moved, not even to turn his head. The silence was absolute.

Then, slowly, fear clear in his voice, one of the men said, "Speak again."

Ken said quietly, "I am an officer in the United States Navy. I need your help."

The men murmured in their own language and, slowly, one by one, turned their heads toward him.

Ken took another step forward. "Believe me," he said.

"We cannot see you," a man said. "Will you come closer?"

"If you intend to harm me I will not."

The man with the watch said in a deep, honest voice, "We intend no harm."

Ken moved closer to them. Then, taking off his dog tag, he said, "I swear to you that I am an American. Here." He threw the dog tag on the ground near them.

The man with the watch picked it up and held it face to the sky. " 'Kenneth Malcolm Braden, USNR,' " he read out loud. " 'Oh two seven six five six three.' " He held it out and Ken strung it back around his neck.

"How did you come here?" the man asked.

"That isn't important now," Ken told him. "I need your help."

Another man said, "We can't help you. We can't even help ourselves, for we are dying here." He came close to Ken. "Three days ago my son, my little son, picked up one coconut—just one small coconut—and started to run home with it. He stumbled and fell against the fence and it killed him. Just a little boy."

"I'm sorry for you and your wife," Ken said. "What is this fence?"

"The Japanese have made a fence of wire which goes completely around their place. If you touch it you cannot turn it loose before it kills you."

"It is electrified," the man with the radio said.

"Are their buildings inside this fence?"

"Yes, all of them."

The man who had lost his son said, "We can't help you. Go away the way you came before you cause great trouble for us all."

"What help do you need?" the man with the watch asked.

"I want to get into the building where the Japanese radio is."

"That cannot be done. Not only is there the fence, but there is also a guard at that building both day and night."

A man asked, "How many are with you?"

"I'm alone," Ken told him.

"*Alone?* Then you can do nothing."

The man with the watch said, "Come with us, for we have been here too long."

Ken followed the group as it moved silently through the jungle.

When they reached the village the man with the watch, who, Ken guessed, was the leader, ordered the fire to be put out.

The women, glancing at Ken over their shoulders, hurried, pouring sand from their hands on the fire.

Darkness settled over the dark people and the dark houses.

A man touched Ken lightly on the arm and said, "Come."

Ken knew now that he had gone too far with this thing ever to turn back. If he had misjudged the honesty and the feelings of these people he was lost, for there was no alley of escape.

They led him to the largest of all the houses. It was raised up from the ground two or three feet, and as Ken went into it, he felt the woven mats of coconut leaves under his feet.

The thin leaf walls let in only the faintest light from the stars—just light enough for him to make out the upright posts which supported the thatched roof and some low benches along the walls and down the center of the single large room.

He could hear, behind him, the bare feet of many people moving as the man with the watch led him down the length of the room. "Sit here, please," the man said.

Ken sat down on the low bench in the center. Shadowy people sat along the walls, but only one man sat on the bench beside him.

The man with the watch said slowly, "This is why we cannot help you, sir. When the Japanese came here they divided our island into two parts. One is theirs, one is ours. They can come whenever they wish into our part, but we cannot go at all into their part."

A voice from the darkness said, "Nor can we fish, even in the lagoon, from our boats. Nor even gather the coconuts and breadfruit which grow on their end."

The man beside Ken went on, "The Japanese have already killed a great many of us. They don't care whether they kill men, women, or children. If we break the smallest of their many laws we die. To help you attack them could only end in the death of all of us."

"I intend no attack," Ken told him. "All I want to do is to get into the radio building—alone—for a few minutes. All I need from you is information. Is the fence guarded with sentries?"

"No. That fence needs nothing more than the death in its wires."

"How many men are in the radio house at night?"

"One. Sometimes two, but usually one."

"Does he sleep during the night?"

"No. He listens. Someone listens there all the time."

"Then different men come during the night?"

"Yes."

"Would it be possible to get this man out of the house for a few minutes?"

"I do not think so."

Another man said, "It cannot be done."

But the man with the watch said, "When the supply ship comes many of the Japanese get drunk. Perhaps then the American could get into the house?"

"Perhaps," a man agreed.

"When does the supply ship come?" Ken asked.

"About once a month. It should be back here in a fortnight or less."

"Do the men in the radio house get drunk then?"

"Some do, some don't."

The man who had lost his son said from the darkness, "That is the worst time for us. They come into our village and beat or kill us if we try to stop them."

Ken stood up. "I would like to ask for only this much help. Please don't let the Japanese know that I have been here. If you think that any of your people would tell the Japanese about me, ask them not to do it. Tell them that I am trying to do something which will bring the American Navy and Marines to this island much sooner—if I succeed. If I fail because someone tells the Japanese, we will be delayed in saving you for months, perhaps years."

"No one will talk about you," the man with the watch said. "No one."

"Thank you."

A voice asked, "Tell us, are the Americans losing the war against Japan?"

"No," Ken said. "We're winning it. We have stopped their advance in the South Pacific and we are now moving against them in the Central Pacific. We're moving toward you island by island. This is the truth, no matter what the Japanese tell you. We are coming."

"We will try to live until you reach us," the man beside him said. "But already the old ones and the children are dying for lack of food. We cannot fish for we have no hooks, no lines, and the Japanese have ruined our boats and nets."

Ken stood up in the darkness. "I will come back tomorrow night with hooks and lines. Will some of you—just a few—meet me on the south end of the island at midnight?"

"I will come," the man with the watch said.

"And now," Ken said, "I ask that you do not follow me. I ask this only because if you don't know how I got here the Japanese will not be able to torture you until you tell them."

"We will not follow. God go with you, sir."

CHAPTER 4

FOR SEVENTEEN OF THE LONGEST DAYS in Ken's life the *Shark* patrolled the entrance to the lagoon. All day long it lay motionless, a hundred feet below the water, the motors stopped, while it listened—in vain—for the sound of the supply ship. At night it lay surfaced in the entrance, the radar antenna always turning and searching.

During this time Ken went back to the island and the starving natives several times. On his first trip he took them all the fishhooks and lines he could find in the *Shark's* emergency kits and from the crew's tackle. On another trip he took them as much condensed milk as the submarine could spare, warning them not to let the Japanese see the empty cans. He took them dried eggs and evaporated potatoes and a little meat. Shelton, the radioman, let him have some emergency batteries for their radio.

He also took them the news that, after the bitterest and bloodiest fight in the history of the Marine Corps, they had taken Tarawa and the Gilbert Islands.

Ken had also, in the light of the new moon, seen the Japanese installation on the northern end of the island. There was a long, wooden building which was apparently where the soldiers slept. There was another, smaller building which, because naked men came in and out of it, Ken decided, was a bath. The generator for the transmitter was in a low shed, open to leeward. There were two gasoline motor generators mounted side by side in it.

The transmitter building was farthest from the barracks, being at the base of the mast. It was a one-room house, quite small, with two windows and a door. Often the man on watch there sat in the doorway with the headphones on.

The electric fence was more than six feet high. It was mounted on wooden posts and glass insulators, and constructed of web wire so that a man could not go through it. Ken assumed that it was hot all the time for one or the other of the generators was always running, even, the natives said, in the daytime.

There was no open approach to the transmitter shack from the north for the Japanese had built the electric fence all the way around their buildings, leaving only one wire gate on the southern side. This, too, was hot, Ken guessed, as the wire was set off like the rest on insulators.

The Japanese had not cleared a path for the fence but had run it through the jungle, crookedly to avoid the big palms. Then they had simply cut away the undergrowth for a foot or so on each side so that no leaves or branches could reach the fence and short it out.

If they had cleared a wide area on each side of the fence Ken's plan would have been much harder. But, as it was, there was jungle on both sides, the only real clearing being around the buildings and along the paths between buildings.

Although seventeen days of patrolling were a misery to the men in the *Shark*, they gave Ken time he badly needed.

The days below the surface were hard on the crew. The boredom ate into them so that men lost their tempers and fought in the cramped spaces. Monotony and heat and foul air frayed and drained them, and the lack of sunlight turned them a ghastly, grayish white, so that, as they moved slowly around, they looked like bloodless ghosts. Once, because two men could not settle their differences, Carney let them fight it out on the foredeck.

Many of the crew came up to watch it, standing in silence in a ring around them and with only the light of half a moon on them. It was a mean, savage fight, but at the end the two felt better and within a few days were friends again.

There were no shovels in the *Shark* but there were paint and bilge scrapers and other tools which could be used to move dirt. These Ken took ashore.

And so, night after night, a line of the dark-skinned natives approached the electric fence. Then, in the thickest part of the jungle, they disappeared.

Inch by inch they dug into the ground. The dirt they moved was passed out behind them and carried by the women to be scattered thinly under the brush.

Ken went often to help them and to measure the progress of the tunnel. It was large enough only for one man to crawl along it as it went down on this side of the fence, leveled off for ten feet, then turned upward again.

At last, when a bilge scraper broke the surface on the other side of the fence, Ken called a halt, leaving the earth undisturbed over there.

They concealed the open end with trash and fronds, brushed away their footprints, and settled down to wait.

Seventeen days of a blank radar screen, of only the sound of fish in the sonar headphones.

And then, at eleven in the morning of the eighteenth day, the soundman said, "Slow screw bearing three six zero, distance ten thousand."

"Good," Carney said. "Take her down to a hundred and fifty. Rig for silent running. Do you hear any sign of sonar?"

"Not yet, sir. Just one slow screw. Sounds like a light ship of some sort. Not a can."

Carney plotted the range and bearing as the soundman kept reporting. "It might be what we're waiting for. She's headed straight for the lagoon. Any sonar?"

"None, Captain. No pinging of any sort."

"Let's keep it quiet in the boat."

"Steady at one fifty, Skipper," the Diving Officer said.

"Hold her there and shut down everything."

It grew very quiet in the *Shark*. And, almost instantly, very hot as the blowers and fans stopped.

Now, through the hull of the ship, they could all hear the slow, steady *chug chug chug* of the propeller above them. It grew louder and louder without changing speed at all, then, slowly, it faded away until only the soundman could still hear. "Screw slowing," he reported. "Now she's stopped."

"What's the range and bearing?" Carney asked, then plotted them. "She must have anchored close in to Midnight, and at the northern end. Boy, I'd love to take a look, but we'd better wait. Start fans and blowers and come up to sixty feet."

The soundman said, "I hear something but it's hard to make out what it is. Sounds like high-speed screws, but very light."

"What's the range and bearing?"

"Same as the slow screw, sir."

"They must have put a motorboat over the side to take supplies ashore. Do you still hear it?"

"Yes, sir. Very light high-speed screw."

Ken said, "I hope they've got a boatload of sake and barrels of brandy. I want them to have all hands drunk as skunks up there tonight."

"Pity you can't get in there and give 'em all a Mickey Finn," Pat said. "Slip something in that sake that'll knock 'em *all* out."

Ken turned to him. "That's the best idea you've had since you made lieutenant, Lieutenant. What have we got?" He swung down the ladder from conn and went aft to where the Pharmacist's Mate kept the ship's supplies of medicines. "Doc," Ken asked him, "what have we

174

got that I can put in a bottle of sake that'll put a man to sleep—but not kill him?"

Doc scratched around in his uncombed hair. "Let me see, let me see, Lieutenant," he said, unlocking the cabinet. "I've got some sodium barbital. How'll that do?"

"What is it?"

"Sleeping pill."

"What does it taste like?"

Doc rolled a pill out and let Ken taste it. It had only a slight bitter taste.

Doc began reading from a book. "Says here a dose of three to ten grains induces drowsiness within an hour or so and then a satisfactory period of natural sleep should ensue. The effect lasts from six to eight hours and there aren't any unpleasant aftereffects."

"What would happen if you doubled the dose?"

Doc kept on reading. "Fifty grains and he's a dead Japoon."

"What would twenty do?"

"Let me see, let me see," he said, reading. "Here we are: too much and, instead of sleep, you get loss of consciousness or coma."

"That's what we want. How about mixing me up a good-sized double dose, Doc? Make it into a powder so I can pour it into a bottle."

"Rodger dodger."

"Wait a minute. Will the stuff dissolve in alcohol?"

"That I don't know. It'll dissolve in water OK."

"Have you got any drinking alcohol?"

"Who, *me*? No, but the captain has."

Ken got a miniature of brandy from Carney and asked him if it was anything like the Japanese drink, sake.

"Sake is a beer," Carney told him. "It's got a kick like a mule, though. Lots of alcohol. They usually drink it hot instead of cold."

Ken took the brandy back to Doc and dropped one of the pills into it. The pill took about two minutes to melt. Satisfied, Ken went back to the wardroom and asked Willy to get him an empty ketchup bottle. Then, while Willy stared at him, he practiced dumping salt into the mouth of the bottle. He would wrap a little salt in a piece of paper and then, by just feeling, he would try to empty it as quickly as he could into the bottle. He got very good at it.

And then he waited. At four-thirty in the afternoon sound reported the slow screw again and the *Shark* went back to a hundred and fifty feet down and silent. Again the screw went over them and faded away.

In Carney's cabin he and Ken went over their final plans.

Ken had seen that the Japanese stood watches just as the U. S. Navy did: four to eight, eight to midnight, midnight to four. He planned now to start for the island earlier than usual and to be all set when the watch at the transmitter shack was changed at midnight. That would give the new watchstander plenty of time to get drunk—if he was going to get drunk—and give Ken four hours before the watch would be changed again.

That done, he spent the final hours getting ready. Into one waterproof package he packed both the Minox cameras and exposure meters. He also packed the two twenty-grain doses of sleeping pills, each separately wrapped so that if he spilled one he'd have a spare. He also packed one of the small metal distress mirrors. Then he checked his Aqua-Lung, rigged a full tank, and gathered up his gear.

At ten o'clock that night he was ready. Except for the first trip ashore, he had not been using the escape hatch but, instead, Carney had been bringing the boat up so he could get out the deck hatch. Tonight, however, they decided not to surface, but to use the escape hatch.

Standing under it with Malone, Ken heard Carney's order to stop engines.

"Here we go again," Malone said.

Ken nodded as he put the Aqua-Lung on.

Malone ran down the check-off list, item by item.

The talker said, "The Skipper says good luck, sir."

Ken put the fins on and opened the lower door of the escape hatch.

Pat said, "This is the big one, Ken. How do you feel?"

"All right."

"No bucket this time?"

Ken tried to grin. "Not yet. But have it ready when I get back."

Malone said quietly, "I've been praying for you, Ken."

"Thanks, Pat. Hope it works."

"Take care of yourself. All the way."

"I will."

Pat looked away for a second and then back at him. "Don't let them get you. Not alive."

"I'll try. Well, so long." Ken climbed up into the escape hatch and put the mouthpiece in.

"See you soon," Malone said, closing the door.

Ken stood there in the absolute darkness and waited for the creak and then the avalanche of water.

He wasn't afraid. He felt no courage, no feeling of bravery, he just simply was not afraid. He wasn't trembling, nor sweating. His mouth wasn't dry, nor his stomach sick.

The water pouring in knocked him to his knees. When it stopped moving he straightened and pushed his way upward.

On the deserted southern beach he took off the gray nylon coverall and wrung the water out of it. While it was drying he buried the swimming gear and unwrapped the package. Then, putting the coverall back on, he slung the two Minox cameras and the meters on their thin chains, and the mirror on a string, around his neck. He put a packet of sleeping powder in each side pocket.

He had come a long way toward the native houses before he heard any sounds of man. But, as he came closer, he could now hear a great deal of noise. People were crying and yelling and the little children were screaming.

He stopped some distance from the houses of the natives and whistled as the men had taught him to do. Soon an answering whistle came and, in a moment, the leader emerged from the bushes.

"They are bad tonight," the man said somberly.

"Are they drunk?"

"Like pigs," the man said in disgust.

"That's bad for you, but it's good for me," Ken told him, then added, "I'm going now."

"I'll go with you. As far as the fence."

"I'd better go alone," Ken told him. "You've done all that you could to help me."

"Will we see you again?"

"Perhaps you won't see me again. But you will see Americans again. Endure this; try to keep alive until we come."

"It's easier to live knowing that. Hunger doesn't seem so savage." The man suddenly smiled, his teeth white in the darkness. "And we are catching fish now. We will live, I think."

Ken touched his shoulder. "That's fine. Good-by, and thanks."

"Good-by, and may God go with you tonight."

Ken kept close to the beach as he went past the village. He could hear the crying of the old women and children, and the coarse shouts of the drunken men. Occasionally, as he moved along in the shadows, he could hear people crashing in the underbrush and he guessed that they were Japanese, as the natives made almost no sound when they moved.

As he neared the northern end he could hear a lot of

noise at the Japanese camp, and when he reached the fence, he could see the Japanese.

Most of the men seemed to be gathered in the barracks. In the bright light he could see them sitting around tables. Many of them were singing, a few were staggering around, and some were lying on the floor.

He went along the fence slowly until he reached the entrance of the tunnel. From there he could look over the jungle growth and see the radio shack. The man on watch was sitting in the doorway, the headphones on, the chair tilted back against the doorjamb.

It was now midnight. Ken checked his watch and kept looking at the man in the doorway. As no one came to relieve him, Ken began to worry. Maybe he had been relieved early. Maybe no one would remember to come.

He could see no sign that the man on watch had been drinking. He certainly wasn't drinking anything now and there were no bottles in sight.

Ken's whole plan was built around the necessity for the Jap on watch to be drinking. If he was not, then Ken would have to make really radical changes in his plans and danger would increase a thousand times.

He waited. Five minutes. Ten. This was time he could not afford to lose. But, he argued, if he started for the shack now, or even reached it and started getting rid of the man on watch, the relief might suddenly show up. Then he would have two Japs to handle. And neither of them must, at any time, see him. How could he do it?

Ken heard loud, drunken singing. He turned his head a little and looked toward the barracks.

A man was coming down the path toward the radio shack. He had an armful of dark green bottles and was singing at the top of his lungs.

The man on watch stood up.

The two met in the doorway and, it seemed to Ken, argued about something for a few minutes. At last the one with the bottles put them carefully down beside the chair.

The argument went on, their voices rising. Finally the newcomer pushed the other toward the path and bawled at him as he walked away.

Ken watched the newcomer put on the headphones, sit down in the chair, tilt back. Then he reached down for one of the green bottles and raised it to his mouth.

Ken said silently to himself, "Drink some more, my friend. Drink some more."

For now it was time to go.

CHAPTER 5

THE MOUTH OF THE TUNNEL WAS SMALL and very black. Ken, down on his hands and knees, suddenly wondered if any snakes or scorpions had gone down into it. The idea made him shiver as he went slowly, head first, into the damp, pitch-dark hole. He slid for a little way and then came to the level section which ran under the electric fence. Now he could see absolutely nothing. Dirt fell on him as he crawled along and the bottom was muddy with rain water. There was a disagreeable smell of something dead in there.

Coming at last to the other end, he pushed gently against the earth above his head. He could feel the tangled ends of wet roots dripping from the topsoil above him.

More and more moonlight streamed in as he gently made an opening in the ground.

The radio shack was ahead and to his left. The man was still sitting in the doorway, the earphones on.

That helped, for Ken could not avoid making slight noises as he crawled, almost on his stomach, through the thick brush.

He headed away from the shack to his right, planning to circle back when he was behind it.

Once he stopped because of a sudden increase in the noise the Japs were making, but it was only a bunch of drunks bawling at the closed gate.

Going on, he soon found that he could no longer see around the corner of the shack, so that he could not tell what the man on watch was doing.

He went faster now as he reached the cleared area around the foot of the transmitter shack. Light streamed from one window in a broad, faint band, stronger than the moonlight. He got in close to the house and, almost touching the wall, crept to the corner.

The man was still sitting there, the chair tilted back.

Ken watched the yellow hand reach down for a green bottle standing a little apart from the others. The man's back was to him as he drank and put the bottle down again.

It was still half full. Ken got a packet of the sleeping powder and opened it, pinching the paper to form a little funnel.

His practice with the ketchup bottle came in handy. The white powder poured into the neck of the sake bottle without a grain touching the glass.

That done, he lay down close to the side of the building and watched.

It was half past twelve.

Soon the yellow hand came reaching down again, feeling for the bottle. This time the man held it in both hands, spinning it slowly back and forth as though warming it.

Ken waited, hardly breathing. The man was clumsy and, at each turn of the bottle, came close to dropping it on the concrete stoop.

At last he raised it, still holding it with both hands, and drank.

He drank long and deep and then, instead of putting the bottle down, he held it for a while in his lap.

Then he drank again, this time emptying the bottle. Ken couldn't see what he did with it but guessed that the man had put it down on the floor of the shack on the other side of the chair.

Then he picked up another of the long, heavy bottles and pulled the cork out with his teeth. The sake foamed thickly over his hands and down on his clothes but he seemed either not to notice or not to care. He started drinking again.

He drank steadily. At five minutes past one he began to sing softly to himself.

At fifteen minutes past one he nodded, his head going down on his chest. But he recovered and pulled the cork from another bottle.

At one-thirty his head fell straight down on his chest, his arms dropped down beside the chair, and his legs sprawled.

Ken, watching him, waited for five minutes but the man did not move again.

He moved behind the chair and touched the man lightly on the back of his neck. There was no reaction at all.

At one thirty-six the man's breathing became noisy—a dry, steady snoring.

Ken picked up one of the full bottles and, still creeping, the bottle held ready by the slim neck, he went around the man's limp feet and into the shack.

He put the bottle on a shelf and, for an instant, looked around. Dead ahead was a shelf with a transmitter-receiver reaching from wall to wall. On the shelf to his left there was an old typewriter. To his right there were what looked like comic books, old newspapers, some dirty dishes and cups, and a rusty stove.

There were, as far as he could see, no books, nor any sort of coding board or machine.

Feeling a sick rush of disappointment at the lack of any sign of a code, he went on with his preparations.

First he set the little metal mirror on the door hinge so that, just by turning his head, he could look into the mirror and see all the way down the path to the barracks.

Next he got both Minoxes and the meters out from

under his coveralls. With them dangling around his neck, he took one step over to the shelf with the radio gear.

There was not a single piece of paper with writing on it. Lying in front of the receiver was a pad of cheap ruled paper without a mark on it and, beside that, two or three yellow pencils, all sharpened with a pocket knife.

He turned to the shelf with the comic books and dishes. He went through the old, tattered papers swiftly. There was nothing.

One of the comic books showed a U.S. sailor on a battleship. On the sailor's chest was tattooed another battleship. Then a Japanese battleship appeared and sank the U.S. ship, blowing the sailor up into the air. While he was still in the air a Japanese main battery rifle shot a hole in him, sinking the ship tattooed on his chest.

Ken didn't think it was very funny as, almost desperate now, he turned back to the transmitter shelf.

He went through the pad of paper page by page. They were all blank. Then—why, he could never explain—he lifted the hinged metal lid of the receiver.

Pasted inside the lid were long strips of paper covered everywhere with ideographs. The first thing he recognized was a column of numbers. Opposite them were two more columns of ideographs, only some of which he knew.

There were two electric lights in the shack, one overhead, the other a gooseneck lamp. He brought the lamp over and twisted the shade so that all the light fell on the strips of paper pasted on the lid.

Then he checked the mirror.

For an instant his heart stopped. His breathing stopped.

A Japanese, in uniform, with a cartridge belt and holster, was walking down the path toward the radio shack.

As he passed what Ken thought was a bathhouse another man came out. The two talked for a moment, then the first man came on.

For what seemed like centuries Ken couldn't even make his mind work. He just stood there, paralyzed, his hand on the shelf holding him up.

Then, gradually, his mind began to work again. The first and most important thing was not to be seen.

But there was no way out of the shack except by the single door. The windows had been screened simply by nailing the wire over them.

He was trapped there in the shack. For a moment he felt panic coming up solid in his throat.

Then he accepted the fact that he was trapped and put it aside.

He took one quick step and picked up the full bottle of sake. He held it in his right hand, by the neck.

He was now standing opposite the man in the chair which faced the barracks. Thus he could see the man coming down the path, in the mirror above the drugged man's head.

It was two o'clock in the morning. Ken noticed that now things were much quieter. Only a few tuneless strains of singing came from the barracks and these were almost drowned out by the sound of birds and bugs and the wash of the sea on the windward side of the island.

The walking man's feet made a soft, swishing sound in the cloth sandals he wore. If he had been drinking there was no sign of it for he walked without any staggering or weaving along the path.

His image in the mirror grew larger and larger until at last it was just a blur of grayish uniform.

Then Ken saw one of the curious sandals swing into his area of vision. The sole was made of layers of cloth and a short length of padded rope came up between the big toe and the next one, thinning out into a cord

185

which went around the yellow ankle and held the sandal on.

Then the trousers and, at last, the man.

He stopped—about two feet from Ken—facing the man in the chair, and said something. Ken could not understand the words but the tone was angry.

He said the same short sentence two or three times. Then he reached out and slapped the man's face with the palm and the back of his hand.

Then, just as Ken had done, he walked around the sprawled legs and entered the radio shack.

What happened then was, to Ken, a strange, unreal thing. Even as it happened he felt as though he were watching this event at a movie or on a stage and that the people taking part in it—himself and the Japanese soldier—were only actors.

It was unreal, too, in that it seemed to him that the whole thing took a very, very long time. Although he knew in a part of his mind that only a few seconds went by, it seemed to him that hours—*years*—were spent there.

He felt no fear whatsoever. In fact, he felt nothing at all personal. No fear, no regret, no feeling of sympathy, nor of compassion, nor of achievement.

It was, simply, an act which had to be done. Although he had not included this thing in his plans, now that it was here it had become a part of them and, like getting the tunnel dug, it had to be done.

The Japanese looked straight at him. First he looked into Ken's eyes and then his own slanted eyes flicked down to the cameras hanging from the thin chains. Then they moved back to Ken's face.

The movement had started long, long ago and, it seemed to Ken, it went on, and on.

The green, heavy glass bottle had a nice feeling of balance in his hand, of weight and leverage. If he had swung it straight down it would have felt even better. But he did not swing it that way for, a long time ago—

a second—Ken had realized that nothing short of killing the Japanese would do.

So he swung the bottle sideways, aiming for the little sunken place in the yellow skin just beyond the left eye.

The Japanese was moving his hand toward the pistol hanging in the cloth holster from the cloth belt when the bottle got there. Ken had swung it with all his might and, at the end, had added speed to its movement by snapping his wrist into it.

The green bottle broke just beyond Ken's fingers and the man's skull broke also.

Before he could fall Ken took him by the shoulders and shoved him back out past the sprawled legs. Then he let him fall slowly on the concrete, his head lying in a pool of foam and blood.

The pulse in the yellow wrist went on for a few seconds and then stopped.

Ken took one long, deep, shivering breath through his open mouth. Then he looked again into the mirror. The path was empty now.

Going back to the receiver, Ken checked his exposure meter readings and began photographing the strips of paper glued in the receiver. He used different exposure times and lens openings, different lighting angles and distances, and used both cameras.

When he was through he closed the lid and put the lamp back where it had been. Then he made a final and thorough search but found nothing else.

Going over to the drugged man, he pulled the earphones off and threw them on the floor. He then pushed the man out of the chair and rolled him half into the room. Taking the broken sake bottle, he put the neck of it in the limp hand and made it stay there.

The trip back to his buried gear Ken never could remember. He saw no one, heard no sound of man.

At the beach, ready to start for the *Shark*, he whistled

once—the signal that he was through. It was answered from far away and, as he walked into the water, he was sure that, already, the natives were filling the tunnel so that, by dawn, there would be no trace of it.

As soon as it was deep enough Ken went under water. Then, staying only a few feet below the surface, he watched his compass course and the time.

It was three-thirty.

When he guessed that he was within a hundred yards of the *Shark* he went deeper, stopping his descent when he was forty feet down. Then, still on the compass course, he swam slowly.

There was no light from the world of air and land, so that, actually, he could see nothing. But there in the water were a million lights. Some drifted, pale, pale green and faint; some moved like shooting stars; some were only twinkles and flashes. All pale and deathly faint.

When he thought he was close he stopped breathing so that the exhaust from the Aqua-Lung wouldn't drown out all other sound. Now he could hear noises coming from the sub. He had gone a little to the left of his course, so he turned now and headed straight for the sound of low, slow machinery, of an occasional dull bang of metal against metal.

He ran into the rough steel side of the *Shark*, scraping his wrist against her.

Feeling his way along, he found the conning tower structure above the deck. Floating beside it, he got the knife and began hammering on the steel.

In a moment he heard answering bangs from within the ship.

At last, the cameras safe in their waterproof cases, Ken stood in the blackness of the escape hatch.

Then the water dropped away from around him and light streamed up.

He looked down between his legs and saw Pat Malone's great black beard and the scar on Carney's face.

It was like coming home after a long and dangerous time.

CHAPTER 6

IN WILLY'S SERVICE PANTRY IT WAS HOT and dark and, after two hours of being shut tight, smelled badly. Ken wiped sweat off his face as he pulled the long, thin strips of film out of the wash water and started drying them.

Here on these little strips of film was either the success or failure of his mission. Here, perhaps, was the secret which would save ships and men and time in this war against the Japanese. Here was what he had risked his life for.

And killed a man for.

As he carefully dried the strips he felt the angle of the deck tilt down and heard the roar of the diesels stop.

Dawn.

Dry at last, he opened the door and wiped the sweat off his face.

Carney was waiting in the wardroom.

Ken put the first film into a battery-operated viewer which magnified the frames about twenty times.

There, the writing white, the background black, the negatives sharp and clear, were photographs of the strips of paper pasted in the hinged lid of the transmitter. With a flood of relief, he handed the viewer to Carney. "At least I got pictures," he said, "but I don't know what of."

"They look clear," Carney agreed, "but meaningless."

Ken looked through the viewer for a long time, sweat beginning to run on him again. At last, he pushed the viewer over to Carney. "Do you see those columns in dot-dash code? It isn't Morse. But do you notice that, starting with the right-hand column, the dots and dashes change under each column?"

"Yes, they do."

Ken got the dictionary and began looking up the ideographs at the top of each column. "They're phases of the moon."

"Say that right-hand column is the basic code," Carney suggested. "The one coming in from Pearl. Then, with each phase of the moon, the island operator would shift to the code under that phase."

"Could be," Ken said. "Or it could be just—nothing at all."

"How long will it take you to break that down into a message we can send?"

"All day, I should think," Ken told him.

"All right, we'll set up to send it as soon as we surface tonight. But why don't you get a little sleep before you tackle it, Ken? That must have been quite a party last night."

Ken glanced at him. "I wonder if I killed a man for—nothing."

It was a long day. In the first place, Ken couldn't sleep. For almost an hour he tried, but whenever he felt drowsy he would begin to remember the tunnel, the shack, the green bottle, the eyes of the Japanese man just before all expression went out of them.

Giving up, he went to work translating the columns into English. That done, he spent the rest of the day in the hot radio shack encoding the message for Pearl.

As soon as the boat surfaced that night Carney came down to the radio shack. When he saw the length of the message he frowned. "That's going to be a long transmission. Hope there's nothing taking bearings on it." He initialed the release and Shelton began tapping it out on the bug.

"Come on down to my cabin," Carney said to Ken.

Ken followed him and willingly sat down on the bed when Carney motioned toward it. Suddenly he was dead-tired, drained out, so tired that he seemed to ache. His brain was so tired that he could hardly make it figure out that he hadn't had any sleep for thirty-six hours.

"What do we do now?" he asked.

Carney didn't answer until he had settled in the single chair and put his feet up on the tiny desk. "Tell me this, Ken," he said quietly, "how did it go?"

Ken told him briefly what had happened on the island. When he finished, Carney just sat studying the ragged sandals he had on his bare feet. Finally he said, "Only two things worry me. I wonder if the natives are going to talk. Maybe a kid will accidentally say something. The other thing is: what are they going to think when they find those two—one dead, the other drugged?"

"That's the *only* thing that worries me," Ken told him. "The natives won't talk. I'm *sure* of that. And no children ever saw me. They hate the Japs too much and we mean peace and freedom to them. They won't talk. Now that other thing: in the first place, no one—except the dead man—saw me. I'm sure of that. So what else can they think but that the drunk (they'll think he's drunk, not drugged) got into a fight with the other guy, smacked him with a bottle, and then passed out?"

"Don't see what else they can think," Carney agreed. He was still studying the ragged sandals, lining up the tips of them and squinting at them.

Slowly through Ken's weary brain he began to feel that something was wrong. Carney was usually perfectly direct; he usually looked at you when he talked to you. So far, Ken suddenly remembered, Carney hadn't looked at him at all.

"What's the trouble, Skipper?"

Carney finally turned his head and looked straight at him. "It's this, Ken. You came back with some pictures. We don't know what they are. They might be nothing at all. We won't know until we get the word from the cryptanalysts in JICPOA."

Ken nodded. He was sure now that something deep and serious was bothering Carney.

"We're going to hang around the atoll until we hear," Carney went on. "In case"—he stopped and looked at Ken again—"we have to go back and look harder for that code."

Ken straightened up on the bed. "I looked pretty hard, Skipper. If that isn't the code then it isn't in that radio shack."

"Are you sure, Ken?" Carney asked. There was no insult in his tone, no meanness. Just a sort of doubt. "Did you look everywhere?"

For a moment Ken just sat there. Then he leaned slowly back and rested. "Phil," he said, "you're thinking about the time I puked in the bucket, aren't you?"

He could tell by Carney's face that he was hating this. "Well, yes, Ken. And you were a little shaky on the bridge that day, too."

Ken grinned. "I sure was. I was scared stiff, Skipper. But I wasn't afraid when I was in the shack. I don't know why I wasn't, I just wasn't. Don't get me wrong, I didn't feel brave, I just wasn't scared. I looked *everywhere* for that code and I left no sign that I had been there." He paused and looked at Carney. "I wasn't scared, Phil. Just a little when I saw the Jap coming, but then only for a second."

You could see Carney relax, see the furrows of strain in his face smooth out. "That was something I had to *know*, Ken. I think I knew it anyway, but I wanted you to tell me. And I just hope you got what you went for."

"*So do I*," Ken said.

Carney lit a cigarette and slipped his feet out of the sandals. "Wouldn't it be nice now if we got word from COMSUBPAC that you'd done your job and, next, that we could go hunting? We've got fuel, food, and fish for a nice little patrol." Then he suddenly laughed out loud. "Boy, I'm *dreamin'*," he said, still laughing.

"Why?"

Carney stopped laughing. "COMSUBPAC wouldn't let me and Frank take his little yacht on a patrol for anything in the world. I'll bet the admiral has gnawed off every fingernail he's got already."

"I don't see why," Ken argued, amazed.

"I'm just temporary skipper. I haven't even passed the qualifications for command yet. I'll bet you a day's pay, Ken—yours against mine—that the next word we get from COMSUBPAC says, PROCEED DIRECTLY TO PEARL HARBOR STOP DO NOT ATTACK UNLESS UNAVOIDABLE STOP. . . ." He was about to go on when Shelton, hardly pausing to knock at the door, shoved the curtain aside.

"Here's an OP priority URGENT for us, Captain," he said, handing Carney a dispatch page and the coding board.

"OP URGENT?" Carney said, his tone changing. "Must be something hot. Maybe I lose that bet, Ken."

"I didn't take it," Ken reminded him as he started decoding the message.

COMSUBPAC SENDS TO SHARK STOP LARGE ENEMY TASK FORCE IN YOUR AREA STOP ASSUMED TO BE EN ROUTE TO ATTACK OUR FORCES IN GILBERT ISLANDS STOP BASE COURSE ONE EIGHT SEVEN STOP RADICAL ZIGZAG ESTIMATE SPEED ON COURSE ONE FIVE STOP POSITION LONGITUDE EAST ONE SEVEN EIGHT DEGREES ZERO FOUR MINUTES ONE ZERO SECONDS LATITUDE NORTH ONE FIVE DEGREES THREE TWO MINUTES ZERO EIGHT SECONDS STOP AT THIS DATE TIME GROUP ZEBRA STOP ESSENTIAL THAT THIS FORCE BE DELAYED OR DIVERTED STOP SHARK ACKNOWLEDGE STOP.

As Ken broke the words one by one, Carney plotted the position. He then advanced it to the present time and called up for the *Shark's* own position. Then, scribbling

194

on the back of the original message, he handed Ken the piece of paper. "Shoot this one out in a hurry."

Carney's message read:

SHARK ACKNOWLEDGES STOP AM ON BASE COURSE DEAD AHEAD STOP ESTIMATED DISTANCE FIVE SIX MILES STOP WILCO STOP.

Fifty-six miles. Speed on course fifteen miles. Three hours and forty-five minutes. It was now nine o'clock.

As Ken began encoding the message he wondered what was going to happen.

As soon as Shelton had gotten the message out and an acknowledgment from Pearl, Ken went up on the bridge to find Carney.

The bridge was crowded with Pat, Si, Bill Adams, a doubled lookout section, and the talker.

"Pearl just said 'a large task force,'" Carney was saying. "So I don't know what's in it. Perhaps troop transports going down to attack the Marines on Tarawa. Maybe heavy stuff going down to soften the island up before the attack troops get there. Might be nothing but a fishing fleet."

"How'd they get picked up?" Pat asked.

"Must have been one of our patrol planes out of Midway."

"Hope the Japs didn't spot him and change course," Si put in. "We're really set for him right here."

"Maybe a carrier," Pat said. "Oh, how I'd love to sink me a carrier."

"Whatever it is, we'd better get ready for it," Carney told them. "If there're any destroyers we'll get a working over just as soon as we shoot—maybe sooner. Get everything secured for depth-bombing. Check your emergency lights and CO_2 absorbers. And, Frank, get all the loose gear stowed so there won't be a lot of stuff flying around hitting people. Bill, put three engines on the batteries and bring them up as high as you can. We've still got two or three hours to go, so jam it into those batteries. Get all hands fed—good—and let as many men hit the sack as you can spare. Let's put Chief Milton in the forward torpedo room, Chief Johnston, aft, and let Madden have the wheel when the time comes. Who's the best soundman?"

"It's a tossup between Swift and Keller," Pat told him.

"Make it Swift. Keller had the mid-watch last night. Now let's ride the vents and wait for them."

Officers and men disappeared from the bridge. Ken stayed and told Carney that the message had been received.

"Thanks," Carney said. "Well, it's a nice night for a fight. In this moonlight we've got a chance of seeing him before he sees us."

"What's going to happen?" Ken asked.

"Not sure. If it turns out to be a real task force they'll have a screen of destroyers all around. We'll have to get inside the screen before we can get a shot at the big boy—whatever it turns out to be."

"Then what?"

Carney chuckled. "Shoot at everything in sight and then run like a homesick angel. Which won't do much good because the Japs are smart. In the early days we could take everything they had standing on our heads. They used to set their depth charges to explode at two hundred feet, so all we had to do was go down to three hundred and silently steal away. But some blabber-mouth newspaperman published a story about it, and within two weeks the Japs were dropping them right down the chimney. They can get rough."

"What's it like to be depth-charged?"

Carney laughed but he didn't sound happy. "The waiting is the hardest part, I think. You're down there in the water and you don't know what's going on. Then, without any warning at all, the thing explodes. If it's a long way off you hear a 'click,' if it's close you don't—just the biggest noise you ever heard. You'll go through one tonight, Ken. You'll see how all hands look to see if water's coming in or air's going out. They look *hard*." He swung around. "Let's take a look at the boat. Things should start popping around here pretty soon."

Ken followed him down the ladder and on forward to the torpedo room. It was quiet in there, most of the men in bed, the lights dim. Carney talked in a whisper to the chief and Si Mount, and then inspected the tubes.

As Ken stood in the dim darkness he was still haunted by the fear that he had accomplished nothing on the island; that the pictures were only of someone's doodling.

And now, he thought, with this fight coming up, we'll be submerged, so there won't be any radio reception. Maybe, he thought, I'll never know, never find out.

He shrugged off the idea and followed Carney aft.

Bill Adams, who was now Engineering Officer, was standing beside the panel with its yard-long bright metal levers which controlled the electric motors. As Carney came up, Bill tapped the faces of some gauges on the bulkhead.

Here, too, the light was dim and there weren't many men on watch.

"Topping off now," Bill said. "They've got about all they can hold."

"Keep pouring it in until the last minute," Carney told him. "We might need every amp we can get."

Then he went on aft to the stern torpedo room. In there a few men were making final adjustments while the rest slept.

On the way back to the bridge Carney said, "We're about as ready as we'll ever be." Then he turned and smiled at Ken. "This is the first time I've ever fought a boat as Skipper."

"How does it feel?"

"Terrible. Being commanding officer sounds good— back in Pearl. Out here—well, if I make a mistake a lot

197

of people get hurt. Good people. I never knew before how lonely the commanding officer is."

Carney climbed back to the open bridge. "What's the word?" he asked Pat.

"Nothing yet, Skipper."

Carney looked at his watch. "Midnight. We've got about forty-five more minutes if their speed on the base course is right."

"Bridge! Bridge!" The voice was urgent.

"Bridge, aye, aye," Carney answered.

"Something on the screen, but can't tell what it is." Carney dropped swiftly down the ladder.

In the darkness Pat said, "This is it, Ken."

"You think so?"

"Bound to be. They're moving faster along the base course than we thought."

"What does that mean?"

"They're zigzagging—going right and left of a line which is their base course. Say, they're making twenty knots through the water and zigging back and forth—that'll move them along the base course at only sixteen or seventeen knots."

"Wonder what it is?"

"I want a carrier."

Carney came back up the ladder. "Lookouts, what do you see?"

"Nothing yet, sir."

"There's something dead astern of us," Carney told them.

"What does it look like, Skipper?" Pat asked.

"Big. They're still too far away for the blips to separate, but I'd guess that there are a dozen ships in the group." He dropped back down the ladder.

Soon his voice came up the tube. "He's zigged to the right now. Looks like eight small ships and three big ones."

Ken heard the driving diesel speed up and then felt

the submarine turning. Looking aft, he could see the white, curving wake as the *Shark* came around a hundred and eighty degrees.

"Hold your hat," Pat said quietly. "Here we go."

Nothing happened for almost ten minutes. Then Carney said, "He's turning to his left. Time of zig ten minutes even. You should see him soon."

The driving diesel slowed, but the other three kept on charging the batteries at high speed.

"Object dead ahead," a lookout cried.

Carney came instantly up the ladder. Putting the big night binoculars in the rack of the target-bearing transmitter, he swung it ahead. For a long time he looked, and then straightened up. "See if you can make him out, Pat."

Malone stooped to the eyepieces. In a moment Ken heard him draw in a quick, sharp breath. "One destroyer. Another can. A cruiser or a big can. Can't be sure. That's a carrier. It's a *carrier*, Skipper. Another can. Another. Another cruiser or big can. I'd say cruiser. Another can." Malone straightened. "That's the biggest carrier I ever saw."

Carney nodded. "Clear the bridge," he said.

In a few seconds the Klaxon was sounding. Ken dropped down into the conning tower with the rest and stood back against the wall as the small room filled up with people.

"Hold her at forty feet," Carney ordered. "I want a lot of scope going in."

"Steady at forty."

"Up periscope."

As the periscope moved upward, Carney took the handles in both hands and stooped to the eyepieces. On the other side of the scope Pat Malone took his place as range and bearing reader. He put his hands down on top of Carney's on the handles, which, by turning, Carney could adjust the scope to read off the bearing and distance of the target.

Carney said, "Bearing ... *mark!*"

Malone read out the bearing on the ring above him to Frank Doherty, who was running the target data computer.

Carney said, "Range ... *mark!*"

Malone read the range from the other dial and Frank entered it into the computer.

"Down periscope."

Carney straightened. "Here's the picture. He's in a rectangular formation. Two destroyers are out front, two on each flank, and one or two—I can't be sure— astern. Inside the destroyer screen there are two cruisers. One is a little ahead of and to port of the carrier, the other to starboard and a little astern. The carrier is a whopper."

The soundman said, "Target turning."

"Right on time. Pat, give me a course to get him broadside on."

Pat spun the dials of the Is-Was and read off a course.

"I'm going to slip in between the lead destroyers and the flanking ones and shoot before they pick us up. The carrier is the main target, then the cruisers. Are we set?"

"Set, Skipper," Doherty said.

"Up periscope!"

CHAPTER 7

Now THE *Shark* WAS THE HUNTER, the killer. In a little while, defenseless, she would become the hunted.

As the hunter she was ready. In the conning tower Carney had his eyes to the periscope sights. On the other side of the oily tube Pat Malone, with the Is-Was hanging by a string around his neck, moved as Carney moved—it was almost a dance. The helmsman stood solidly, feet apart, both hands on the brass spokes of the wheel. The radarman had his face down close to the long black cone at the bottom of which glowed the greenish dial of the radar. The soundman sat hunched over listening through the headphones. Hanging to a hook on his table was another set of headphones. Frank Doherty stood beside the target data computer. The correct solution light—a red F—glowed brightly. Standing out of the way was the telephone talker with the rubber-padded earphones and a little curved bucket-like thing around the mouthpiece so that he could talk into it without disturbing the others in conn. A young sailor, still too young to shave, stood by as messenger.

Down in the control room two men, both stripped to their shorts, sat facing the wheels and holding two great bronze wheels. One of these controlled the bow planes, the other the stern planes. In front of each man was a bubble level. The Chief of the Boat stood in front of the control panel, with its levers and wheels. Above him the "Christmas tree"—a panel of lights which showed whether every opening in the hull of the *Shark* was closed or open—glowed green—the green board—

except for one red light down in the corner. Thus all openings in the hull were closed. Along the bulkheads across from the planesmen more men stood ready at banks of wheels which opened and closed vents and valves, controlled high- and low-pressure air, and made it possible for the boat to become heavier than water, or lighter. Back in the engine room the four great diesels were still and silent, the heat from them hanging heavy in the room. Now the electric motors were turning over with the high-pitched whine. Controlling these with the rheostats feeding more or less power from the rows of batteries which lay below the deck for almost the entire length of the boat were the electricians under Bill Adams.

In the torpedo room forward the ready lights glowed on the six bronze-capped tubes.

All hands in the boat were silent. There was no kidding, no horsing around. No talking at all.

Now everything—the target, the killer, the sea—had become a problem in simple arithmetic. The target was traveling at high speed on a straight line. The submarine was approaching that line at right angles. Now the problem was to get the torpedo to a place on the target's path at exactly the same instant the target got there.

Since the torpedoes were, compared to bullets, exceedingly slow—traveling about thirty miles an hour—it would take them a minute to go half a mile, a thousand yards. Therefore you couldn't hit the target by shooting straight at it but, with arithmetic, you could find the course to put the torpedoes on so that, while they ran along their path, the target would run along *its* path, and, if your arithmetic was right, torpedo and target would come together at a point in the open sea.

The torpedoes, powered by electric motors and steered by small gyroscopes which held them rigidly on whatever course they had been set to, were designed to explode either upon hitting a ship or, if they missed, to explode magnetically as they went under a ship.

A problem in arithmetic.

Through the periscope Carney could now see, outlined by the moonlight, the carrier. Planes, their wings folded upward, crowded the immense flight deck. Ahead of the carrier was one cruiser; astern, the other.

Swinging the scope around—Carney and Malone doing their weird, slow dance—he saw the lead destroyers far ahead.

The two flank destroyers filled the field of the scope and were coming straight at him, their bow waves smooth white slices in the water.

"All ahead flank! Pour it on 'em, Bill," Carney ordered. Then he spoke to the people in conn. "Two of the cans are barreling right at us. Don't know whether they've spotted us or not, but we want them to pass astern."

The soundman plugged in the loud-speaker so that they could all hear the noise of the target propellers. The carrier and the cruisers made a deep-throated *chug chug chug* while the destroyers came through with a high-speed *thrum thrum thrum.*

"Bearing . . . Mark."

"Range . . . Mark."

"Down periscope. What's the distance to the track?"

"Two thousand, Skipper."

"Torpedo run?"

"Two six six oh."

"Are we ready to shoot, Frank?"

"Outer doors still closed, Captain."

"Up periscope."

Carney swung the scope all the way around, a full three hundred and sixty degrees—Malone in the solemn dance. Then he signaled for the scope to go down by flipping up the handles. "We're inside the screen. The two cans haven't changed course, so they must not have spotted us. Let's take the sea pressure off and get the doors open, Frank. All ahead one third."

In a moment the talker reported that the outer doors of all torpedo tubes were open.

"All ahead full. Give the lead cruiser one fish and one for the stern cruiser. Then put a four-fish spread into the carrier. Set depth twelve feet. Set speed high."

In seconds Doherty was giving the talker the gyro angles to be set on the torpedoes.

In only seconds more the talker reported depth, speed, and gyro angles set on the six torpedoes forward.

Carney said quietly, "This is a shooting observation. Up periscope. Bearing . . . mark . . . range . . . mark. *Shoot!*" He snapped the handles up as Frank flipped a switch on the number one torpedo tube board to ON. "FIRE!" he shouted. The talker leaned on the firing key.

The *Shark* lurched as three thousand pounds of torpedo were rammed out of her by compressed air.

Frank made a swift adjustment on the angle solver and then, watching the flicking hand of his stop watch, cried, "Fire two!"

The *Shark* lurched.

Down in control men jumped to valves and levers, letting more water into the tanks to balance the air which, after firing the torpedoes, was sucked back into the boat, so that there would be no impulse bubble rising to the surface to mark their position.

"Fire three!"

". . . four!"

". . . five!"

". . . six!"

Over the sonar loud-speaker they could hear the torpedoes leave the tubes, making a noise almost like a cry of sorrow.

Carney put the scope up for a second, brought it down.

Doherty in a monotonous, toneless voice—as though

nothing was happening—read off the seconds of the first torpedo's run. ". . . nineteen . . . eighteen . . . seventeen . . ."

Pat Malone looked at Carney's face, waiting for the next decision. What, he wondered, was Carney going to do? Was he going to turn hard right and try to run under the stern escort of destroyers, hoping, in the confusion (if there was any) not to be heard going under? Or was he going to swing all the way around and try to escape the way he had come?

Carney's face told him nothing. It was calm, studious, waiting, as Doherty counted the seconds.

Doherty said, with no emotion whatever, "Missed the lead cruiser. Here's number two." He began to count again. ". . . four . . . three . . . two . . ."

WHRANNG

The sound went all through the boat as though someone had suddenly pounded on it with an immense hammer.

"A hit," Doherty said calmly. "This is number three. Four . . . three . . . two . . . one . . . one . . . two . . . three . . . Must have gone under him . . ."

WHRANNG

Four and five missed.

Six hit the trailing cruiser.

"Up periscope!"

Carney and Pat danced.

Then orders began to snap from Carney. "Down periscope! *Take her down—deep!* Rig for silent running."

Then he turned to Frank and grinned. "Beautiful shooting, Frank. One cruiser is dead in the water. The carrier is a bonfire."

"Can't see how we missed that first cruiser," Doherty complained.

"He had dropped back and was sheltered by the carrier. We might get another shot at him later."

The soundman said, "Sonar sounds, very mixed, sir."

Carney put on the other set of headphones and listened intently. "Either the cruiser or the carrier is breaking up. Neither is moving." He took the phones off. "At least one destroyer sounds like he's found us."

The deck of the boat stayed at a steep angle as it dove for the depths, the gauge unreeling.

While they were waiting, everyone watching the depth gauge, the talker said, "Radio reports that just before we went under he got a message for us from COMSUBPAC, sir."

"Ask him if we're the action addressee, and what's the priority?" Carney asked.

The talker reported in a moment, "Radio says no action required by us and priority only routine."

Carney nodded. "We'll decode it later. Level off at three hundred."

Then he turned to Doherty. "Don't you think, Frank, that if we stay in close to the carrier we've got a better chance of not being picked up? There's going to be so much noise coming from the cripples we'll be hard to hear and the cans will expect us to make a high-speed run away from here."

"I think it's our only chance, Skipper."

"Three hundred feet, sir."

Carney nodded. "Run at silent speed. Stop blowers. Stop ventilators. Turn on emergency lights and stop generators. Patrol quiet."

One by one the many sounds in the boat ceased. The whine of the engines dropped to a growl and stopped. The rush of blowers and fans died away. The busy little sound of the electric generator stopped. Men with nothing to do got into their bunks. Men who had to walk anywhere took off their shoes and either went barefoot or put on sneakers. Tools and other metal things were handled with extreme care so that they would not be dropped or otherwise make a noise.

It was very quiet except for the sounds from the surface coming through the loud-speaker and a gentle swishing noise as, running silently, the propellers barely kept the boat moving.

The talker said, his voice low as though he was afraid it would carry up through the three hundred feet of dark water, "Forward torpedo room requests permission to reload."

"Not granted," Carney said. "It'd make too much noise."

"Not granted, Chief," the talker said, almost whispering. "Make too much noise."

A voice from control said, "We're going down slowly, Captain. Want to let in some air?"

"Not yet. Wait. But not deeper than three hundred and fifty."

Just as the soundman started to say something Ken heard from the loud-speaker a faint sound. Far, far away, it sounded like a single tiny tinkle—a ping.

"Sonar sound, single, approaching," the soundman said. "Low-range sound. He's slowing down."

The sound from the loud-speaker grew steadily louder. It was an irritating, annoying, constant thing.

Peep . . . peep . . . peeep . . . peeEEEP . . . peEEEEP . . . Then fading away.

Carney unconsciously looked upward. "He went right over us."

Doherty said hopefully, "But he didn't change his rate."

"Coming back," the soundman said.

Peep . . . pee*ep* . . . pee*eeep* . . . PEEEP PEEEP PEEEP PEEEP PEEEP. . . .

"High frequency," the soundman said as the peeping seemed to search all through the boat.

Carney said quietly, "We're tagged."

"It was bound to come, Skipper. Those eight Japanese

207

destroyers aren't going to let us knock off a carrier and a cruiser without getting sore about it."

Malone suddenly laughed, short and quietly. "Oh well," he said, "we deserve a going over. There they were, bucketing along to beat up our Marines on Tarawa and we stop 'em in their tracks. We deserve a few ash cans."

Carney looked at him and grinned.

The peeping came back, faded.

Ken watched the red second hand on the bulkhead clock moving along with a steady, irritating nervousness. When it reached twelve the minute hand jumped forward.

It was now ten minutes past one o'clock in the morning.

Suddenly, with no warning, no preparation, there was a loud, hard, metallic *CLICK*.

Ken looked at the others in the conning tower. Every face changed, grew suddenly older, more serious.

He couldn't help saying it, although his lips were stiff. *"What's that?"*

Pat Malone just looked at him with somber eyes.

Then it came.

WHAM WHAM WHAM WHAM WHAM WHAM WHAM WHAM WHAM WHAM WHAM.

CHAPTER 8

FOR KEN THE NEXT LONG HOURS were terrible. He thought, many times, as they dragged on, that if he could survive them nothing in life could again be as horrible as those hours in the cold, dark depths of the Pacific.

The *Shark* was heavy. As each torpedo had been fired the water which had replaced it in the tube had been drained out into the forward torpedo room bilges. At three hundred and fifty feet down the pressure of the sea against the hull of the boat was now around three hundred million pounds. The stern tube packings, the sea valves, and other openings in the hull could not stand the torture of this enormous pressure, so that, in many places, the sea was entering the boat—sneaking in like the enemy it was—and adding pound after pound. Like a thief, it was stealing the boat's buoyancy.

"We're about four tons heavy, Captain," Doherty said, whispering.

Carney nodded and tapped the inclinometer. There was a fifteen-degree up-angle on the boat, slanting the deck so that it was hard to keep on your feet.

"Don't you think we'd better pump now, sir?" Doherty asked, his voice low and anxious.

Carney shook his head. "Make too much noise."

The talker said, "Engine room reports bilges full and running over around the reduction gears, sir."

Carney reached for the phone. "Bill? Get a bucket brigade going. Dump the water into the after torpedo room bilges. No noise."

The soundman, who had cut off the loud-speaker at the first click, now turned it on again.

The conning tower pulsed with the *thrum thrum thrum* of the Japanese destroyers' propellers.

The soundman said, "Sounds like they're in a circle, with us in the middle, sir."

With the thrumming came an almost steady peeping from the echo-ranging gear.

"Hard right rudder," Carney ordered.

The boat swung slowly, as though moving in tar.

Then one set of thrumming screws came closer, louder. The peeping rose in intensity until the soundman reached up and turned off the loud-speaker.

Then it was silent.

The soundman said, "He's right on top of us now, sir."

Carney nodded. "You'd better take those phones off, Swift, or you'll get a busted eardrum."

The soundman took the phones off and laid them on the narrow shelf in front of him.

"Rudder amidships."

"Rudder amidships, sir."

The *Shark* turned sluggishly again.

It did no good. As the first depth charge exploded it sent a concussive wave outward. This wave struck the *Shark* with a loud CLICK.

WHAMWHAMWHAMWHAMWHAMWHAM . . . on and on and on and on.

Ken had been looking at a pipe painted green which ran along the overhead of the conning tower. When the explosions struck the boat the pipe vibrated so wildly that it could not now be seen at all.

Men were knocked down all through the ship. The air became gray with dust and paint and cork. Things were torn from racks. Deck plates and gratings—heavy metal slabs—rose and danced, the noise of their clanging unheard, overwhelmed by the tremendous sound of the explosions. Tools and spare parts flew around, deadly missiles in the gray air.

At each *WHAM* the very sides of the boat contracted, moving inward, then bouncing outward again.

The lights went out, leaving only dim light from the battery lamps. Light bulbs all through the ship shattered, sprinkling thin, hot glass everywhere.

Slowly the sound subsided, the air fell back to the deck and became clearer. Men groped their way up to their feet and stood, wondering if they were still really alive; wondering if the *Shark* was still a complete hull in the cold and pitch-black depths of the sea.

Carney, in falling, had cut his head and now blood was running down through the sweat on his face. The young sailor got a rag and helped Carney tie it around his head.

The soundman picked up the earphones and listened again. "They've got us boxed in, Captain."

Blood had soaked through the rag but was no longer running down Carney's face. "When the next one breaks off to make his run, let's try to sneak out through the hole he left in the circle."

Doherty nodded.

Ken looked down at himself. He had on a khaki shirt, khaki trousers cut off above the knees, and sneakers. He was completely soaked with sweat.

So was everyone else. If a man walked sweat oozed out of his sneakers and ran over them to the soaking deck.

Pat Malone came over to stand beside Ken. "Very smart cookies—up there." He jerked his thumb up.

Sweat was dripping steadily from the point of his black beard.

"How much of that can we stand?" Ken asked.

"They're getting close."

The soundman said, "One is breaking off, Captain."

"Give me a course!"

"Two seven oh."

"Steer two seven oh! All ahead flank!"

The boat swung faster this time, with full power on the propellers. Carney put on the other phones and listened, his face intent, his eyes without expression.

Suddenly he turned and snapped, "*Stop engines!*"

He took the phones off. "Didn't work," he said calmly. "They filled up the gap with two other cans. Must have figured we'd try a sneak-out like that. They were waiting to nail us."

"He's overhead," the soundman said.

It was six o'clock in the morning.

This, Ken thought, is the most horrible part of it all. This standing here, leaning forward against the up-angle of the deck; this waiting. Up there, the destroyer, moving in the clean air and brilliant colors of dawn, moving in the realm of the earth man was designed to occupy, was now dropping the barrels into the sea. Ken could imagine them sinking, maybe spinning end for end as they came down, maybe just rolling smoothly. But coming down—down out of the bright surface of the sea, down through the green light, down into the blue, then the deep blue, the dark purple, and into the black. Coming down with, inside them, the firing mechanism preparing itself, the pressure plate coming closer and closer to the trigger.

And there was nothing a man in a submarine could do except pray. Nothing but wait and pray as the barrels sank toward him. Wait, and hope that they wouldn't be so close as to crush in the black hull, and crush out his life.

This time forty-eight depth charges racked the *Shark*. Her hull rang as though pounded by sledge hammers; it whipped as though flexible, and twisted as though in mortal agony.

The young sailor who had given Carney the rag vomited on the deck, and as the spasms racked him, he

212

looked up with streaming eyes at Carney, as though asking his pardon for doing such a thing; and asking Carney not to think him a coward simply because his guts were filled with fear.

As the giant pounding ground to a stop and the needles of the dials ended the wild, quivering dance, everyone looked at some indicator, some mechanical thing which would tell him that the *Shark* was still alive. Carney looked at the depth gauge. The Chief of the Boat looked at the Christmas tree. Men at valves and packings looked to see if wild water was flowing in.

The *Shark* had, somehow, survived again.

Carney helped the sailor to his feet and poured some salt tablets into his hand.

The talker said, "Divisions report only minor damage. After auxiliary panel went out. They're looking for the trouble, sir."

Carney turned to Ken. "Would you mind going aft and see what's going on, Ken?"

"Aye, aye, sir."

He pulled himself up the steep slope to the ladder and went down it.

At the foot of the ladder he stopped in his tracks.

The *Shark* was almost unrecognizable. Slabs of insulating cork had been ripped from the overhead and lay everywhere. Paint had been peeled off. Everything usually stowed in orderly rows and racks and brackets lay all over the deck in a tangle of tools and gear.

On the deck itself was an inch-deep slime of oil and sweat and vomit and water, a filthy, greasy, nasty-smelling gunk through which he had to wade.

At the great bronze wheels of the bow and stern planes, sailors, almost naked and dripping sweat, strained to keep the planes pressing against the sea. A man could stay on the wheels for only a few minutes at a time, so a line of sailors stood, dripping, waiting to relieve.

As Ken sloshed his way aft he noticed that the auxiliaryman and the trim-manifold man had their tools lying on the deck instead of in racks.

It was quiet down there, almost silent. The men, if they talked at all, spoke in whispers.

They were now strangers to him. Their faces were drawn and their eyes vacant. Many looked on the point of collapse as they shuffled dismally in the dim light.

Aft he found that when the distribution board circuit breaker had blown—shooting sparks all over the place—the electrician had yanked open the depth-charge lock-in switch, turning off everything aft. The only light now came from a few battery-powered lanterns.

In the gloom he could see a line of men leading from the engine room to the after torpedo room. In the silence, and silently, they were passing buckets of water from the engine room bilges to the torpedo room, and passing the empty buckets back.

Further aft he found a working party with a hand lamp fumbling around in the slime on deck. The chief, covered with the mess, finally straightened up, holding a piece of wire in his hands. Somehow the insulation had been torn off it and the bare wire had fallen into the gunk.

At the panel they cut out that entire circuit, and soon the lights came on again.

Back in the conning tower he reported to Carney and then took up his station aft, out of the way.

The attack upon them went on, methodically, hour after hour. At irregular intervals a destroyer would break out of the circle which kept them trapped. It would pass directly overhead, as though it knew *exactly* where they were, and then the depth-charges would pour down upon them.

By the end of the day men were beginning to fall and not get up. Their mates would let them lie there, only seeing to it that their noses and mouths were clear of the deepening slime on the decks. Now, on the plane wheels, no man could endure for more than four or five minutes but had to be relieved before he fell, exhausted.

By midnight the air in the boat was so foul that each light seemed to be shining in a grayish fog. Breathing was hard, each man gasping rapidly. Faces were becoming faintly blue. No one smoked for there wasn't enough oxygen in the air to sustain a flame.

"Test atmosphere," Carney said when the *Shark* had been below the surface for twenty-four hours.

In a moment the talker, listless against the bulkhead, suddenly straightened, his eyes scared as he reported, "Carbon dioxide two and a half per cent, Captain."

Pat Malone, standing beside Ken, groaned and whispered, "At three per cent we pass out. At four—we've 'ad it."

Carney ordered, "Open all oxygen bottles and spread all CO_2 absorbent."

And the long night went on, shattered hour after hour by the hail of depth charges.

Nothing the *Shark* did—no twist, no turn, stopping, starting—*nothing* she did let her escape from the trap of the circling destroyers.

And hour by hour the air in the boat grew fouler and less able to sustain life. Men could now no longer stand up but lay on the deck, where the heavier oxygen settled, gasping and, when the depth charges roared around the boat, almost drowning in the horrid slime flowing back and forth over them.

"Atmosphere tests two point eight," the talker said, trying to keep the phone out of the gunk.

Carney slowly got up to his knees. He could barely speak, his voice hoarse and halting. "We're done for. They've got us and they know it. They won't leave us alone until either they can no longer hear us or we surrender. We have two choices—go up and surrender, or go below the cold zone. This boat wasn't designed to go that deep and the chance of coming up again isn't good. Let's think it over awhile."

But then a barrage of depth charges assailed them, crushing in the sides of the boat, ruining the lights.

When it was at last over, Ken whispered to Pat, "What's the cold zone?"

"It's a layer of cold water so dense that the sonar beam can't get through it."

"How far down is it?"

Pat turned his head slowly. Above the jet-black beard his face was now blue, his eyes bloodshot and dead-looking. "Very," he said.

Carney pulled himself to his feet and clung to the periscope tube. "What shall it be?" he asked, breathing deep between each word. "Who wants to surrender?"

The sick young sailor held up his hand. But then he looked slowly around at the others and slowly brought his hand down again. Then he began to cry.

Carney smiled at him. "You answered the wrong question, son," he said. "Who's for the cold zone?"

Hands went up slowly, just raised and lowered.

"Ken?" Carney asked.

Ken had not thought that he was involved in this. He stared stupidly at Carney.

Carney smiled, his blue lips terrible-looking. "It's your life, too."

Ken raised his hand and let it fall.

"All right," Carney said, turning on the mike. "We're going to try to get below the cold zone," he told the boat. "All hands go to your divisions. Close and dog all compartment doors. Rig for very deep running. Each compartment report any serious leaking. Good luck."

The tilted deck, for the first time in hours, came down to level. Then, slowly, it dropped, tilting slightly downward.

The hand of the depth gauge began to move: 370 ... 380 ... 390 ... 400 ...

The soundman tried but could not get up into his chair. Carney, barely able to walk, got over there and turned on the loud-speaker so that they could all hear the steady *thrum* and *peep* of the destroyers, endlessly circling, endlessly tracking them.

The depth gauge hand kept moving down.

Ken had heard the *Shark* crying during the depth charging. Her voice was almost human in its agony.

But now she cried in greater pain. As though the bones of her skeleton were being broken, she made sudden and awful cracking sounds; she groaned and sobbed as the pressure of the dark sea grew greater by millions and millions of pounds.

Pat, lying on the deck beside Ken, crossed himself slowly as the needle of the depth gauge reached the limit of its travel.

The *Shark* went down and down and down. Suddenly Ken saw a thing that fascinated him. Somehow, in the center of the room, the deck was rising up above the level of the slime. Watching it, he couldn't understand it. But there it was, a hump of the deck above the gunk.

Then he did understand it. The pressure on the hull was now so great that it was buckling the deck in the center.

And down.

Carney's voice sounded far away as he whispered, "Listen."

The peeping of the enemy sonar had changed in tone and in loudness. Now it was a dim, faint, plaintive *pip pip pip.*

And, as they went on down, the peeping grew dim, diffuse, irregular.

Then it stopped.

"This is a good boat," Carney said, as though to himself.

The temperature was now a fantastic one hundred and forty degrees. The bulkheads were literally running with water. Ken's vision was so blurred that when he heard Carney's voice and tried to look at him Carney's figure seemed gigantic—it seemed to fill the whole conning tower—a huge, dim, soaking—majestic—figure.

"Level off, Si. All ahead a half."

"Atmosphere tests three per cent, Captain," the talker said. "Sixteen men are out cold."

Carney only nodded.

The boat crept on, slow against the enormous pressure.

"Forward torpedo room reports only one man on his feet, Captain."

Carney nodded again.

The talker said, 'The Chief of the Boat is——" Then he slumped over.

Carney pulled his head up out of the slime and took the phones off, putting them on himself.

As though in a dream, Ken heard Carney say, "Stand by to surface."

The deck tilted upward, sending a wave of the terrible ooze flowing down on him. He pulled his head up above it and then pulled Pat's up too.

Soon, through the sound loud-speaker, they could hear a faint, steady roar. For a long time Carney stood listening to it and turning the dial of the sonar.

At last, in a whisper, he said, "*Thank God*. Rain."

The roar of the rain grew louder and louder as the boat crawled up from the depths.

Carney stopped it at sixty feet and raised the periscope. After walking it all the way around, he said, "Can't see a thing. Raining hard. Down periscope. Bring her up until just the bridge hatch is clear so we can get some air."

Ken heard the water sluicing off the bridge and then the hard, almost metallic pounding of the rain.

"Open the hatch."

Air—cold, wet, sweet air—poured down. Rain—to them like a shower of jewels, like life itself—fell on them through the open hatch.

The radarman said, "Bogey, Captain. Distance ten thousand, bearing one eight two."

Carney, the blue draining from his face, turned to Doherty. His eyes were, for the first time, hard and cold. "Bring her up. Open main induction. All ahead flank."

"What are you going to do, Skipper?" Doherty asked.

"First," Carney said, "let's get some more water between us and those cans. Then we'll recharge batteries for the rest of the night with all engines. Then we'll go back and knock off that cruiser we missed."

Ken heard the main induction slam open and then the pulse and roar of the diesels starting.

The talker, his face still faintly blue, said, "Radio reports a dispatch, Captain. We're action, urgent."

Carney turned to Ken. "Can you break it, Ken?"

"Aye, aye, sir."

In the radio shack Ken worked the coding board. The urgent dispatch read:

SHARK PROCEED TO PEARL STOP TRIGGER AND SEA WOLF NOW ATTACKING CRUISER YOU LEFT STOP NICE SHOOTING CONGRATULATIONS STOP.

Ken phoned that one up to the bridge.

He was suddenly so tired that he could barely keep his eyes open. Thinking hazily back, he realized that for more than seventy hours he had had no sleep at all.

As he started to get up, Shelton pushed another message toward him.

He had completely forgotten that one. Slumping down again on the wastebasket, he went to work, the slides on the board hard to move with his listless, clumsy fingers.

Slowly the message emerged from the meaningless code groups:

COMSUBPAC SENDS TO LIEUTENANT (J.G.) BRADEN STOP MISSION ACCOMPLISHED STOP WELL DONE STOP.

The words meant nothing to him at all. His mind, so dulled by exhaustion, could only grasp that the message required no decision by Carney, no action on the part of the *Shark*.

Lurching to his feet, he didn't even see the message fall and sink into the slime as he staggered on to his cabin. With his last measure of strength he climbed up to his high bed and fell into it.

After a while Willy, a trayful of sandwiches in his hands, looked into the cabin. He was about to wake Ken up when Carney came by. "Ssssh," Carney said, "let him sleep."

Willy let the curtain drop back into place. "I hear we're going back to Pearl, Skipper. We through?"

Carney nodded. "Yeah, Willy, Pearl. He did his job."

"I've been wondering," Willy said. "What job did he do, Captain?"

Carney looked at him. "A whale of a job, Willy."